THE

Fear and suspense are the hallmarks in Hugh Scott's thrilling books, which feature the supernatural or paranormal. "Atmosphere is vital, especially in books about the supernatural," says the author. "*The Gargoyle* is not a ghost story but I do hope it's terrifying... I certainly try to make my books scary – it's a good reason for reading a book!"

It was in 1984, two years after winning the Woman's Realm Children's Story Writing Competition, that Hugh Scott decided to give up his job as an art teacher and become a full-time writer. His first novel, *The Shaman's Stone*, was published in 1988 and several more titles soon followed. These include *Why Weeps the Brogan?* (Winner of the 1989 Whitbread Children's Novel Award), *Freddie and the Enormouse*, *The Haunted Sand*, *The Camera Obscura*, *Something Watching*, *The Place Between*, *A Ghost Waiting* and *A Box of Tricks*, as well as two stories for younger readers, *The Summertime Santa* and *Change the King!* (all published by Walker Books).

Hugh Scott is married with two grown-up children and lives in Scotland.

Other books by Hugh Scott

Change the King!
Freddie and the Enormouse
The Summertime Santa

For older readers

A Box of Tricks
The Camera Obscura
A Ghost Waiting
The Haunted Sand
The Place Between
The Plant that Ate the World
The Shaman's Stone
Something Watching

THE GARGOYLE

HUGH SCOTT

WALKER BOOKS
AND SUBSIDIARIES
LONDON • BOSTON • SYDNEY

First published 1991 by Walker Books Ltd
87 Vauxhall Walk, London SE11 5HJ

This edition published 1992

4 6 8 10 9 7 5 3

© 1991 Hugh Scott
Cover illustration © 1995 Bruce Pennington

Printed in Great Britain

British Library Cataloguing in Publication Data
A catalogue record is available from
the British Library.

ISBN 0-7445-2330-3

For Nanna Hamilton

He watches,
but breathes not,
and spits on passersby.

Eighteenth Century tract

If I could steal another man's soule,
I would live his time, and mine.

John Dee, 1564

1

*Marion and Derek explore the loch shore,
and Marion hides her fear*

WEDNESDAY AFTERNOON

The girl sheltered by the stone gatepost. She
peered across the road, but snowflakes veiled
her view of the shore.

She heard water sighing on rocks.

A door clunked behind her, and she pulled
her face tight, blinking snow from her lashes,
snuggling deep into her anorak; wishing Derek
would leave her alone.

He came counting, his voice light and
gleeful.

She stared into the shroud of weather,
savouring her aloneness to the last second. A
remark rose on her breath that would make
Derek retreat. But she closed her mouth. She
was above small cruelties. At least, she wanted
to be.

". . . thirty-four, thirty-five, thirty-six! Thirty-six paces from the door!" he announced. "It was only ten in London!"

"I know —"

"Thirty-six! That's from the front door, including three steps down to the gravel!"

"Thirty-six of your steps," said Marion.

"I wonder how deep it is!"

"Can you hear the loch?" she murmured.

Derek pulled a six-inch ruler from his anorak and plunged it into the snow at her feet.

"Four and a half inches. That's over eleven centimetres!"

"Why don't you get a modern ruler?" Marion gazed at the tumbling white world. "Isn't it beautiful?"

"This was Grandfather's! And Father used it all through his school-days."

Marion smiled, nodding. She knew the story, and treasured the ruler almost as much as Derek. Father called it a scrimshaw, because it was cut from walrus ivory and precisely graded in inches by Grandfather's Great-uncle Morgan.

". . . and Great-uncle Morgan was killed by a whale!"

"Can you hear the water?" whispered Marion.

Derek stood silent, close to her elbow.

"Is the loch deep?" he said.

"Oh, yes."

"It's a shallow beach."

"If you waded out, it would dip suddenly, and you would fall down and down, slowly, the water colder and colder, darker and darker..."

"How do you know?" She felt him shiver.

"We did glaciated valleys at school."

His nudge dug into her hip, and she laughed.

"Let's go onto the beach," he said.

"Aren't you sleepy?"

"I suppose so. But it's too exciting. I wonder how wide it is."

"The road?"

"The loch! Come on."

"Wait." She held him back. "Look at the snow. Isn't it perfect? Like cotton wool. Not a footprint. But it's falling so fast I can hardly see any distance towards the village. But there's a tree on the beach, and long grass following the verge. Listen. Listen."

They stood, chins lifted, blinking at snow-flakes, while the loch mumbled among unseen stones.

"Come on," said Derek, and they spoiled the road with footprints; ribbed prints, Marion saw, cut by their wellingtons. She wondered at how easily people marked the world.

Derek jumped, his head suddenly level with her toes. She clambered onto rocks beside him, and snow hissed as it slipped from the tree's branches. Flat among the rocks, grey puddles sucked down snowflakes.

"Do you like the house?" whispered Derek.

Marion smiled and went carefully over boulders to where the loch lay licking the shore, and seaweed heaved. The water's surface seemed to tilt up as it receded into the rushing daylight. She knew Derek was not asking if the house pleased her; he was asking if it was a good house. She turned, stones clicking under her boots.

Derek stood below the tree, waiting, his blond hair white, his anorak hood crumpled behind his head. She knew he was afraid.

"Oh, yes," she assured him. "It's a good house."

He smiled widely and a little laugh burst from the smile, as if he'd been holding his breath.

"Come here," she said. He walked towards her and she placed her hand on his forehead. His eyes closed, and his smile danced with relief.

"Better?"

He squatted suddenly, searching for a pebble. His arm whipped, and the loch's smooth surface broke and shuddered.

The girl watched, listening. The boy crouched, silence falling around them, rocks in white bonnets; the air rushing in millions of white, light pieces. She closed her eyes, sending her senses along the loch shore, across the narrow road that wandered hand in hand with garden walls. And beyond the walls, sugared lawns and grand stone houses, roofed with slate, weighed down by tall chimneys; and smoke rising, defying the dropping feathers.

"You're smiling," said Derek, and she hushed him with her hand.

She followed, in her mind, the curves of the road, the twist around a rock as tall as a bus; and her smile went limp. Blood ran cool under her skin.

"What is it?" whispered Derek. "Do you see something?"

She opened her mouth. "Oh!" she breathed.

"What's wrong?"

"Oh, no!" she moaned.

"Marion!"

"Daddy!" Her breath went out of her, and she felt Derek's hands on her arm, pulling at her.

"Stop!" he said. "Stop! I hate it! Marion!"

She gasped and opened her eyes.

"Marion!"

In the silence, in the distance, a door opened.

She gazed into Derek's blue eyes. "Don't cry," she whispered. "Listen."

Through the busy white air rose the chill sound of a violin, note upon lingering note, easing across the water, hauntingly beautiful, mysterious as a dream.

Derek rubbed his face with his anorak cuff.

Marion smiled down at him.

"It's all right," she murmured. "Home now."

2

Derek talks too much,
and Marion says more than she intended

Marion gripped Derek by his trouser belt, and hoisted him off the beach onto the white-laden grass. They crossed the road, and laughed as the violin squawked. Marion yelled, "Daddy!" from between the gateposts, and by the time they'd trudged the thirty-six paces – or most of them – Father stood hunched in the porch, elbowing his home-made Stradivarius, eyes tight in ecstasy.

"She saw something," said Derek, and Marion tugged his shoulder. "Well, you did!"

Father stopped playing, and his eyes, suddenly open, struck at Marion; dark blue eyes, alive with understanding.

Father straightened. "Perhaps we'll not tell your mother." His glance shifted to Derek, and Derek hid his face by rubbing snow from his hair onto the doormat.

"And," continued Father, "we will start as we mean to go on in this house." Marion looked at him. "Use the back door," smiled Father. "Wet things in the utility room. Food!"

"Goody!" said Derek, and Marion ran to keep up with him.

They crunched past the lounge windows, pointed like church windows, then down the side of the house between its brown sandstone wall and trees trying on wedding gowns.

At the back of the house, Marion let Derek dash ahead. She lingered, loving the three old clothes poles with pineapple tops and skeleton fingers sticking out to catch the clothes line. Snow whitened the coach-house; the coach-house still to be explored.

She danced on the back doorstep, practising a heel-toe-skip of her tap lesson, but the hollow flop of wellingtons was unsatisfactory – though her dancing had shaken the snow from her boots.

In she stepped, cheerful, through the utility room, into the kitchen with its cupboards under worktops (which Mother adored), and the square table Father had made in London specially to fit this kitchen; specially to please Mother.

"Be sure your hair's dry, Marion," said Mother at the oven, prodding a fork at a coil of Cumberland sausage in a tureen, and glancing anxiously.

Father sniffed as the herby taste drifted through the kitchen. He laid the lid over the sausage and swept the tureen to the table.

"Hands," said Father, and Derek groaned but joined Marion at the sink. Then they sat watching Father's thin fingers slit the sausage into piglets, Mother's chubby fist wiping the ice-cream scoop through mashed potato.

"Yes, please," said Derek, and Marion nodded in agreement at the potato and sausage, still feeling the chill of outdoors.

"It's so snowy," said Mother, and her cheeks shone red with heat. "A change from the summer. Wasn't it hot that holiday! I do hope we can warm this house."

"It's been empty a month, Lizzie," said Father. "Give it a day or two. Oh, and remind me to phone the garage for logs. I don't imagine the coal lorry will get over the hill. Don't you love it already!"

Mother nodded. "But it's so icy out of the kitchen. I don't want the children catching cold –"

"Central heating's on," said Father carefully. "Isn't this sausage something!"

"Good!" said Derek.

"You didn't mind going through the Lakes on the way up?"

"Keswick was lovely, John. I'm glad the snow didn't start until this morning. And the butcher's in Keswick reminded me of Harrods —"

"Marion saw something," said Derek.

Mother's mouth stayed open.

Marion sighed, and glared, and Father's stare caused Derek to sit very still, just his fork tapping at peas.

"Big mouth," said Marion, and Derek stabbed a pea to death.

"I really don't wish to hear," announced Mother.

"The snow was eleven centimetres deep," said Derek.

"Really," said Father, but his gaze held Marion. "You'd better tell us." He patted Mother's hand. "It's always best to know."

Mother sat, her fair hair limp.

"May I finish my sausage?" asked Marion, and she ate, enjoying her food to the final mouthful. "Derek, I would like some milk."

Derek's mouth snapped open and his glance sprang at her, but Marion looked at him, and he rose and brought milk from the fridge.

"Thank you," she murmured.

"There's rice pudding," said Mother. "Good and filling."

"It wasn't too bad," whispered Marion.

"You shouted for Daddy."

"Be quiet! You don't know! You know nothing!"

"Marion!" hissed Father.

."Well, he doesn't!"

"None of us do. Please go on."

She glared at Derek, then remembered she was above small cruelties.

"I – Oh. Daddy?"

"D'you want to leave it until later?"

Marion sighed.

"I sent my mind through the snow. Following the garden walls. The houses stood peacefully, chimneys smoking. Not like in London. Oh, Daddy. There's a rock at the roadside. A huge rock with the road wriggling like a worm to get round it. There's something on the rock. A house maybe, but oh! the emptiness! I met a wall of emptiness. Daddy! Like a gap in the fabric of the world. There's nothing like it anywhere. As if God had scooped away a piece of His universe, leaving Nothing! I almost went into it. It would have been death. Death and terror for ever!"

Father rose and his arms protected her.

"I don't know what it means," whispered Marion. "Do you know?" She turned, her face close to Father's jumper.

"Perhaps it won't trouble us," he whispered.

"Perhaps the sun won't rise."

Mother laid her knife and fork on her plate. Derek's eyes hung blue on Marion, his mouth open. His glance slid to Father then Mother. His mouth closed.

On the cooker, a pot clicked as it cooled.

"It knows I'm here," breathed Marion. "Oh, Daddy!" Her voice shrieked, "*It has begun!*"

3

Marion shivers,
and Father orders a dead man's firewood

"A rock at the roadside," scowled Father.

Mother's brow shone, speckled with sweat. Derek, thought Marion, was a small clone of Mother, with crinkled fair hair and a round face.

"D'you mean the castle?" Father wandered to the cooker. "The road certainly is worm-like. Second gear even in good weather; and the rock hangs out like a fat man's waistcoat. There was nothing wrong last summer? I mean —"

"The castle!" whispered Marion. "I had forgotten —"

"We went up the lane beside the castle because of the For Sale sign. Don't you remember, Lizzie? We considered buying the bally place. Wasn't that what gave us the notion of living here? Then *The Glasgow*

Herald had the advert for the chair at the University... Things came together, eh? So..." He turned to the cooker. "Rice pudding." He served the pudding, bumping gently with the wooden spoon. "The best china," he murmured, his eyes returning, blue and strong, to Marion.

"I haven't found the pink ones," whispered Mother.

"The pink ones hold two extra mouthfuls," said Derek.

"So do you," muttered Marion.

"The castle," said Father, giving the biggest helping to Derek, "is on the rock. Jolly good rice. Carnation Milk?" He poured milk, and Marion ate, enjoying the surprise of raisins. "What do you mean, 'It has begun'?" asked Father gently.

Marion saw Mother's fear, and glared at Derek who was shovelling rice. Mother had never understood. Beyond the kitchen's single window snowflakes hurried down. High on the wall hung a metal question mark, which was a spring holding a brass bell. Marion saw the wire that pulled the bell, lumped with paint, burrowing into the wall. No electricity in those days. The kitchen was hot. Marion rose and put her hand on the radiator. She jerked her palm away.

"Working well?" murmured Father. Derek stopped eating. Mother breathed through

22

her mouth.

"Don't you feel the chill?" whispered Marion. She knew they felt only the heat from Mother's cooking and from the radiators. Heads shook.

Marion opened the door and stepped across the passage to the dining room. The bay window bulged out into flurrying snow. The ceiling was higher than at home in London, and crusty with plaster thistles and roses, blurred with a hundred and fifty years of whitewash.

The fireplace stood taller than Marion, black marble exposing a throat of brick. She walked from wall to wall, touching radiators. Father creaked the door shut, squeezing out Derek.

"Can you feel the cold here?" asked Marion.

Father nodded. Marion glanced at the windows, then wandered to the fireplace.

"You've to phone the garage," she said.

Father waited.

"This cold," said Marion. "It followed me from the castle. When I touched the castle with my mind. It came with me here. It didn't know about us until then. Now it knows where we live. Knows we are new. And about you, and Mother and Derek. There's been nothing like it. Not even in Ireland. . ."

"Is it a problem?"

"Oh, yes." A shiver slithered through

Marion's muscles. She drew in a breath, panting suddenly. She rose above the fear. "It. . . It is afraid."

"Afraid of you?"

"A little. It is like a great cold ghost filling the house. The worst thing we can do is be scared." Marion had no doubts about instructing her father. He was a professor, now at Glasgow University, late of Oxford and London; but his experience of what Marion knew, was always second-hand. "You'd better tell Mother that it's gone. And Derek."

Father nodded. "If fear is our enemy, the less your mother knows, the better. And your brother's capacity for retaining secrets. . . Come and have a cup of tea."

Father held out an arm and Marion went into its embrace. They returned smiling to the kitchen. "All's well," said Father. "Touch of chill-in-the-bones for our Marion. Standing in the snow too long after driving all day yesterday with the removal. I see dozy Derek has slowed to below light-speed. Why don't y'curl up in the armchair in front of the TV? Bound to be some garbage that'll help you snooze. Devil of a day for chopping wood." Father lifted the phone, peered at a scrap of paper, and dialled. "Hello. Hello? Is that the garage? Yes. Got any logs?" Marion poured a mug of tea. "How many? Yes? Well. If I knew what four tons looked like. Oh, I see. Could you send it along today? Ardenlee. Yes, I'll be here. Professor Kent. That's right. Moved in yesterday. Got a what? The line's started crackling. An axe? No – that's very kind. Add it to the bill? I suppose so. Goodbye. Work for Father," he murmured. "Now stop being so mournful, Lizzie. Everything's fine. I'm sure you've plenty to do. Derek's off for a kip, so you'll get peace. D'you want Marion? Well, she can help me. You coming outside? Wrap up, then. Logs will be here soon. The lorry was already loaded, but his customer died –"

"John!"

"It's true, Lizzie. Some old chap faded away in the middle of his cornflakes."

"I'm ready," said Marion, as she zipped her anorak and pulled the back door open. "The snow's thicker than ever! I hope the lorry gets through."

"It's only a couple of miles. This side of the hill, fortunately. Out we go! Goodbye, mother of my children! If we're not back in three days, pursue with huskies!"

"Close the door!" cried Mother, and Marion's view of Mother smiling bravely, was squashed as she pulled the utility room door shut.

Snowflakes battled down. "Goodness!" yelled Father, as he crossed the few paces to the coach-house. He pushed a green-painted door. "I think we'll store the wood here," he gasped. "Stove." He introduced Marion to an iron stove. He looked at the ceiling. "Pulleys." His hand led Marion's eye to the wall. "Blackboards." Two blackboards, just big enough to squeeze in a verse from Wordsworth, were built into the plaster.

"But what are they for?" cried Marion.

"I imagine," said Father, "for keeping a tally of the laundry. This is the drying room. Hence the stove and pulleys. Next door is the washhouse. There's a great brick boiler, and two enormous sinks with a wringer between."

"What's a wringer?"

"You'll see. But first. Junk disposal."

"There's plenty of it," said Marion, stepping around a tea chest erupting with rubbish from a previous household.

"Bags of cement," said Father, then groaned. "Hard as concrete. What's this? Lime-in-a-bucket!"

"Don't swear."

"It's lime in a bucket," explained Father. "The fourth clothes pole. Rusted through at the base. What a weight! And a real live deckchair. Paint cans. Empty. Empty. Nearly empty."

"Where will we put it all!"

"The washhouse. If we can cram it in. Proceed, proceed. The bin men can take it later."

The boiler in the washhouse reminded

Marion of a bloated insect, with its brick dome of a body huddled in a corner, and a brass tap dangling like a green leg. Between two sinks was clamped the wringer, its wooden rollers waiting to crush water from washed clothes.

"More junk," said Father cheerfully backing in the doorway, nose-high with paint cans. Snow whitened the floor. "Pile it in!" he gasped. So they piled in junk from the drying room until their feet had cut a path through the snow, and snowflakes melted on their hot faces. Marion pushed her hood back, and flapped her collar to let her skin cool.

Then a crunching rumbled unseen between the house and the wedding trees, and a lorry blinked windscreen wipers, peering for a place to turn, seeking a dumping-ground for logs.

Father crossed beneath the snow-laden phone cable, and spoke to the lorry's window, pointing at the cable. The lorry grumbled, weaving angry snakes in the ground. A man dropped from the cabin, urging the lorry backwards towards Marion — like a lion tamer with a slow dark animal.

Then the man — smiling at the girl — knocked pegs from the lorry's tailgate, and at his shout, the dark animal reared carefully and logs slid, rolling suddenly onto the snow. Some as big as cartwheels trundled at Marion, making her step back, until they jammed in the white ground.

The man handed Father a paper to sign, and gave him an axe with a handle that soared in a tall swift line.

Then the lorry roared forward.

"Stop!" cried Marion, but it stopped too late, and the cable stretched, pressed by the raised back of the lorry. Snow sprang free. Father ducked as the cable *twanged!* snapping, and snaked wildly, the short end smacking against the house, the long end, coiling far into the garden.

Father groaned. The men eased themselves from the cabin, and stared at the whip mark left in the snow. They spoke to Father, then left, the lorry flattening its back with a sigh, and mumbling round the corner of the house.

The tyre tracks filled with snow.

"Oh, Cuthbert!" swore Father, and Marion smiled with her lips.

A chill grew in her brain.

"Could you carry on carrying the junk?" Father hefted the axe. "While your old man strains a muscle with real work?"

"Daddy..."

Father's blue glance stayed on Marion. Snow sagged on his hat. "Something troubling my favourite daughter?" he asked. "I'll protect you." His face tipped, relaxed, serious.

"That was the phone wire, wasn't it?"

"Mm."

"I felt..." Marion breathed cold air. "Oh. A

bit of a chill. You know."

Father's mouth opened. He walked to a thick log. He dropped the axe, and stood the log on end like a drum.

"This," he announced, "is our chopping block."

He laid the axe on the block, and faced her brightly. She thought he looked very handsome in his sagging hat and his favourite jacket of soft grey leather; still good after ten seasons. "I shall return," he murmured, and strolled into the descending weather.

"Daddy —"

But he was gone.

Marion gazed at the cable hanging on the house wall.

The chill in her mind hardened into icy certainty.

The breaking of the phone line had been deliberate.

4

*Father discusses Truth and Love,
and Sandy talks of death*

Marion looked towards the bottom of the
garden. Trees gathered beyond the hothouse,
like ghosts of giants hiding in the snow-filled
air. The trees were part of a wood that
wandered behind all the gardens.

The men from the garage had not, Marion
knew, maliciously broken the phone line. But
she knew — somewhere in her mind near that
cold fragment of fear — that *something* wanted
the phone useless.

When Father returned Marion was struggling into the washhouse with the last wooden
stake and coils of wire.

"I phoned from next door," said Father. "It
might be days, though, before the telephone
engineer gets through this weather. I say!" He
peered into the empty drying room. "Well
done! Right. Fancy brushing the floor while I

swing into the real work? Or should I brew us a cuppa? OK. You brush. I'll brew. Five minutes."

Marion let the steam of her tea creep up her face. She sipped. Condensation lay wet on the kitchen window. The brass bell hung high and silent, its wire smothered with paint.

"Where's Mother?"

Father's fingers wafted. "Lost."

Marion smiled.

Father was very clever. He was so clever he would admit easily when he couldn't answer a question.

"Were we wrong," asked Marion, "to tell Mother a lie?"

"No."

"You know what I'm talking about?"

"Of course. We told her everything was all right."

Marion nodded. "Isn't it wrong to tell lies?"

"Oh, yes."

"But not wrong to tell one to Mother?"

"Mm."

"That's not possible." Marion waited, but Father drank tea. "Explain," she demanded.

"It's wrong to tell lies," murmured Father, "but it's more wrong to hurt people. If we had told our Lizzie that you'd seen trouble, she'd have been scared to death. That'd be cruel. Love is more important than Truth."

31

"Is it?"

"Yes. Should we reduce Mother to a wrecked jelly, just because we want to tell her you were afraid? Do you care that little?"

"Of course not. But—"

"There are no buts, Marion. The choice is clear: do we care more for Truth, or for people?"

Marion sighed into her mug. "Is there a biscuit? Do you want one?"

She put the biscuit packet on Father's homemade table. "But Truth is important?"

"I suppose," said Father, "the search for Truth is the aim of every right-thinking person. Without it your old father would be out of a job. You finished? That's your second biscuit. Derek will have them counted, you know. Do I chop the wood myself?"

"There's only one axe."

"That's the truth. You set the fires. All over the house. Blast the place with heat. Come on. I'll show you how."

Marion set fires using newspaper from the unpacking, dry sticks from various corners of the coach-house, and coal scraped from the floor of the coal shed. She lit the study fire first (switching off the television to let Derek snooze), and watched the coal's black dust sparkling, and soot glowing on the fireplace walls. She pulled the leopard-skin rug over Derek.

She met Mother, reassuring her, as they perched on the window-sill of the staircase window.

They admired the window's painted glass, and Marion held Mother's chubby fist, making her laugh, as Father would, at the disaster of the blue cable.

Mother giggled into her yellow duster and sneezed.

Then Marion failed to light one fire, where smoke rolled across the carpet. She kicked with her slipper at the kindling until the paper beneath blackened. She decided the chimney was blocked and went to tell Father.

A tall person emerged from the coach-house and raised a friendly salute as Marion stared from the back door. Snowflakes fell singly around Father as he stroked the axe through a log. He saw Marion.

"I'm getting the hang of it! Trick is, to let the axe do the work! This is Sandy from next door. Marion."

Sandy saluted again grinning with one side of his mouth. "Cheers, Marion."

The voice was female. Marion said, "Hello," and looked at the jeans and leather jerkin. Sandy bent and gathered logs. Sandy was Alexandra decided Marion. A long earring dangled, and the small head, furred with brown hair, was a woman's head. And the face, rough-skinned and colourless, was a woman's face.

"I think the back bedroom chimney's blocked," said Marion.

"I'll phone Dan," said Sandy, before Father – who was hugging a chunk of tree to the chopping block – could reply.

"Who's Dan?" gasped Father.

"Slater. Builder. Taxi driver. You name it, old son, Dan does it. Chimney sweep. Any coffee going, young Marion? We've been at this an hour'n'more. Good girl."

Marion backed into the utility room, grinning. She hadn't noticed an hour sliding by. She made coffee, and knocked on the window, beckoning. Father straightened his spine, then disappeared into the drying room with the axe.

Sandy swaggered, with a manly thrust of her jaw, slapping Father on the shoulder, as they crossed the snow; smiling her bent smile.

Mother came in from the passage as Father and Sandy entered from the utility room shaking themselves like dogs.

"Lizzie!" cried Father. "Sandy. She lives next door. That way."

"I'll phone about the chimney, Lizzie," said Sandy, as if she'd known Mother for years. "You joining us for coffee? Sit down. Doing a spot of dusting, eh? Marion, could we have another cup for your mother?"

"Chimney?" said Mother.

"Oh, I must tell you –" Sandy hauled a chair under her jeans and grasped her cup like a beer glass. "I couldn't believe it! Old chap along the road croaked. Died," she explained, lowering an eyebrow at Marion. "George the postman, found him –"

"He ordered logs," said Father. "We've got his."

"Oh? Well... Would you believe, he was sitting on the doorstep –"

"The postman?" cried Mother.

"No, Lizzie. Old Jack Merchantman. Sitting on the bottom step, an inch of snow in his lap –"

"What bottom step?"

"His back door step, Lizzie. George had to leg it over him to get to the phone. Some shock, but not too big a surprise. The old boy had been blue in the nose for years. Heart, y'know. And a temper. Ha! Always on the boil about something! Litter on the beach was his favourite. Then it was dead fish in the loch, but the latest was lights in the castle –"

Marion stared harder at Sandy. Father's blue eyes shone on Marion warning her to stay quiet. His glance slid over Mother, then he relaxed, listening.

"– keeping the old boy awake. Said there

were stinks drifting down the castle rock onto his house on still nights. Bit of an old codger. Told George all about it. But poor George. Got more of a shock –" Sandy helped herself to a biscuit and slid the packet around the table. "Mm. More of a shock than he realized. Well, he had to wait for the police, you see, and even though it was ghastly cold, and dark! at that time in the morning, he didn't like sitting in Jack Merchantman's house. I mean, the old boy's egg was still boiling on the stove and his Rice Krispies soaking up the milk. So George thought: what was Jack Merchantman doing outside anyway? In the dark? Half-way through his cereal? Did he hear something? thinks George. So he steps over the remains –"

"Oh," said Mother.

"– nearly falling, because it was harder getting a leg clear of the old chap going *down* the steps... Anyway, George has a prowl, keeping an ear open for the police, and he finds —"

Marion yelped as the door crashed, and Derek stepped in, staggering with sleep, shy suddenly at seeing a stranger.

"Come in," said Father gently. "D'you want milk? Help yourself. And a biscuit. This is Sandy. This is Derek."

"Hi, Derek. Right. George goes prowling, as I said. The castle black as winter beside him on the rock. Shrubbery, yards deep. And in the

36

snow — anyone fancy another biscuit?"

"What was in the snow?" gasped Mother.

"I'm telling you, Lizzie. George was dead right. There had been an intruder. He found footprints —"

"Had the old man been attacked?" asked Father.

"No, no, John. Nothing like that. You don't understand. Footprints, yes. Very nearly filled with snow, but they were like no footprints George had ever seen —"

"What the devil d'you mean?" cried Father.

"They weren't human," said Sandy.

5

Sandy tells of something strange around the castle, and refuses a demonstration

Snow fingered the window.

Sandy hooked an arm over her chair back. She surveyed the family, raising an eyebrow at Marion.

All she needs, thought Marion, is a curly moustache and a Spitfire. Mother ate a biscuit and reached for another. Father invented a cough.

"Was it a dog?" asked Derek.

"Not a dog, old son. George knows every animal track around here. Said it was more like somebody with bricks tied to their feet, than anything he could imagine. Not human. His very words. By the time he got to me this morning — have you had a gas bill yet, John? Just wait. Poor old George was tottering from his van white as the road. He was half an hour recovering. Not that it mattered for he was late anyway, having to wait for the police. But these footprints..." Sandy leaned over the table as if a secret lingered on her tongue and listeners pressed against the doors. "The footprints shocked him more than the dead man."

She sat back slowly, and Marion saw that this strange tall person – under her posing – was afraid. "Can't you see?" murmured Sandy. She leaned forward suddenly. "A dead man on the doorstep. George stepping over him – but it's the footprints that curdle George's blood. Isn't that weird?"

For an odd little moment, Sandy clasped Father's arm, and became a girl dressed for a man's part in a play; then her chin pushed forward, she released Father, and was Sandy again.

"The obvious question," said Father, frowning, "is who lives in the castle?"

"Oh! Lady Ferguson! One of our oldest inhabitants. Been there forty years or more."

"Didn't she sell the castle?" asked Father.

"Sell?"

"There was a For Sale sign up during the summer."

"Oh! Yes! You're right, John. Absolutely. But it wasn't the whole castle. Lady Ferguson kept the ground floor. Beautiful! So I'm told. The place sold all right. I don't think she needed the money. But it's so big. Her daughter moved out years ago and died eventually. Married some bloke her Ladyship didn't like. The daughter, I mean.

"A German bought the castle. Floats around in a Mercedes. And a young boy. Looks a bit ghoulish if you ask me. Smaller than our Marion there. Thin as a twig. But supposed to be brilliant. And the German. He educates the boy. Don't quite know their relationship, whether he's son or nephew or what. But they stick together. The boy's never out on his own. Sails past staring from that car like a ghost, and the man – wow! He's the size of you, me, Lizzie and the kids all stuffed into one suit! Wouldn't like to meet him on a dark night. Though – come to think of it – that's all anyone *has* seen of him. Maybe he's shy. The kid pops out the car to do the shopping. He looks vaguely familiar – the man, that is. Maybe he's been on telly. It's queer," she sighed, eyebrows level in a frown. "Something George said. I'd noticed it myself, yet... You were here in the summer?"

"Yes," whispered Marion.

"It's alive, this place. Every yard. Fish, of course. The loch plopping with the things. And cormorants and heron. Hawks hanging from the clouds; eider-ducks all along the beach; foxes, deer, bugs, butterflies. Teeming life, and all that, but..."

Sandy's frown became anxious. "I noticed

... why, a stillness. It didn't dawn until George said. It lies around the castle. Like a blanket you can't see. Muffling the lochside. Really!" she whispered. "A blanket. There's another rock – or I suppose the same one as the castle sits on – but it makes a promontory into the water. The road winds between it and the castle rock. You could sit there from dawn to dusk pulling in dogfish, rock cod, even salmon if y'cast a line far enough. Now there's nothing. It's like fishing in the bath for all the living things y'see."

"He's talking about the castle," said Derek.

"She," corrected Sandy. "Never could stand long hair and frilly things. But, I say, I hope I'm not scaring you. Some chaps get the creeps with talk like this. Not superstitious are you? You're a bright sort of bloke, John. Not superstitious –"

"Father's a professor," said Derek.

"Huh! Should've guessed! There you are then. No nonsense in this family."

"Actually," said Father. His dark eyes held Marion, and she raised her eyebrows as if to say, "She might as well know now, as later."

"Marion is psychic."

"Psychic? Gets spooked about things, you mean?"

"I mean psychic," said Father.

Sandy shrank slightly, her confident sprawl of limbs contracting.

41

"She is clairvoyant and clairaudient," murmured Father. "Sees and hears at a distance," he explained. "Ninety-four per cent accurate. Our Department of Parapsychology was most upset when we left London."

"Huh," said Sandy. "I say. Dead serious, you are."

"Oh, yes."

Sandy's pale eyes blinked at Marion, then looked away. Under the dry skin of her face, muscles jerked nervously.

"We don't encourage her," said Mother loudly.

"Kind of hard to believe." Sandy's voice rose as shrill as Mother's.

"She could prove it," said Derek.

"No!" hissed Mother.

"Oh, no!" Sandy's furry head turned swiftly to the window. "Time to go! Thanks for the coffee!"

"Thanks for your help," called Father as the guest retreated. "With the logs."

The back door banged.

"Well," said Father. "*Nunc Dimittis*."

"That shut her up," said Mother, and everyone looked in surprise.

6

What came out of the darkness

Beyond the hothouse, night swallowed the trees.

Chimneys stood dimly on the soft roof of the coach-house. In the glow from the kitchen window, cut pieces of tree squatted like strange animals listening for snowflakes.

Marion and Derek carried the coal bucket up the stairs past the painted glass window, into Marion's bedroom. They stoked the fire and shut the curtains against the cold.

Father crept in. "You two warm enough?"

"No," said Derek.

"Not really," said Marion.

"There are heaps of blankets and duvets. Electric blanket on? It's a big room. How about pulling the bed nearer the fire? Not tidy, but it may help."

"I haven't got a fire in my room," said

Derek. "The chimney's blocked."

"He can sleep with me."

"Oh. Good idea." Father moved the bed. "Not too close. We should have a fire-guard, really. How about that? You finished with the bucket? The fire's blazing nicely."

"I was keeping some coal for later," said Marion.

"Quite right. Your old father didn't want to go out again, to the coal shed. There's not really enough in the bucket anyway. Or the coal shed. You keep it, daughter, and I'll chance the frost-bite."

"It's not that cold!" laughed Marion.

"Probably warmer in the coal shed." Father shivered and touched the radiator as he neared the door. "Well. It's on. Remember to wash the hands. And faces. Teeth. Goodnight. Try to sleep. Mother and I will be pottering for a while yet."

"Goodnight, Daddy."

The door closed.

The children used the washhand basin in the bedroom, Marion supervising teeth-cleaning. They changed into pyjamas.

"Put a jumper on," said Marion.

"I'm going to bed!"

"You'll be cold without it."

"Who was that funny person?" asked Derek from inside the mask of his jumper.

"Sandy. She lives next door."

Derek's fat cheeks plopped free and he scurried into bed – the side nearest the fire. "I thought it was a man. She's quite tall, and she's got a man's name. Ooh! The bed's warm."

"The blanket's off now. The flex won't reach."

"Hurry up."

"I'm going to the loo." She went onto the landing.

Doors looked at her. A light in the hall below, glowed on the stairs. Marion could have switched on the landing light, but chose not to. The stair carpet, rather ragged, (left by the previous owners) was rough on her feet.

She opened a door and stood gazing into Father and Mother's bedroom. Their fire made shadows shiver under the bed. More shadows stood behind the curtains, their toes showing.

Marion went to the bathroom, listening to the house, sending her mind up the attic staircase into the little junk rooms. Then beneath the rafters. A plastic basin lay among the joists. Snow dripped from a nail in the roof into the basin. The basin's rim curved imperfectly, part-melted into a blob by a past accident.

Marion drew in her exploring thoughts, washed her fingers, and returned to the bedroom. Derek slept. She snapped the light switch and crossed to the bed. Derek's crinkled hair straggled, yellow in the firelight. Marion found a brush in her suitcase, and knelt, watching the flames and the black-lit darkness of the hearth. She brushed till her scalp tingled.

She wondered why Sandy had escaped after Father said *Marion is psychic*. She could find out.

Her mind stood between the end wall of the house and the night-time trees. The snow had stopped. Shrubbery guarded the house next door. Demanding privacy.

Marion returned to the fire. Her feet were numb with cold. She held them near the flames, then paced to the window. It wasn't right to know too much.

Moonlight whitened the lawn. The thirty-six steps to the gateposts lay thick, without a footprint or tyre track.

Beside the loch, the tree waited, naked but for its soft frock of winter; and the water lay dark, polished by the moon, merging into the gloom of the mountains; and the mountains slept beneath a clean black sky.

Beyond the corner of the garden, towards the castle, an old-fashioned lamp post spread yellow light on the road and onto leaves of rhododendrons in the garden. Marion smiled. Despite the cold, she felt welcome in this house. It would love her, and her family.

She watched the road, staring through the glare of the street light. Had something moved?

A hare? She waited, scarcely breathing.

Something popped up from the beach and ran below the lamp post. Marion's eyes were too dazzled by the light to see clearly. She hesitated about sending her mind to explore. Privacy. It didn't seem fair to spy, even on an animal. And she was slightly afraid. She remembered the footprints that had shocked the postman at the old man's house. Something darted, running fast from under the tree on the shore to vanish behind the garden wall.

The chill in Marion's feet climbed up her legs. Clammy hands touched her back. The hair on her neck tried to rise.

The running things were not animals. What they were she couldn't make out. Another came loping from the direction of the castle, a blob of darkness on the centre of the road. Other blobs followed, running; certainly no bigger than hares, but with elbows, it seemed, jabbing back like men running; dark men running, determined. At the gatepost a shadow broke and a small piece paced along the drive. From the darkness of the beach, up onto the road they came, little horrors, brown, she thought, and shining, as if sweating. Between the gateposts they ran, spreading across the lawn, glimmers of bracelets in the moonlight; using hands and feet to climb the three steps from the lawn up to the gravel patio. Pouring towards the house.

Coming to get her.

7

Marion discovers that Father told the truth about lies; and Lady Ferguson does not send an invitation

A cry closed Marion's throat.

Her heart panicked. She tried not to believe in the moving hoard, trying to think *fact!* not imagination. *Think!* Things running. Dark sweating men. Doll men. Hastening up the walls. *Think!* There's no such thing! Her glance jerked to the outside window-sill.

A hand pawed the edge, miniature fingers sunk in the snow, minuscular tendons rising like wire through the skin, straining –

Then she realized. "You forgot to leave footprints!" she gasped. She pressed against the window. "You forgot to leave footprints!"

The hand was suddenly still.

Moonlight spread bright on the lawn. The running shapes ran, it seemed, into another dimension, vanishing.

The window-sill was a pad of crystalline

white – unbroken.

Marion shuddered.

She pushed back through the curtain, found slippers, and huddled at the fire, rubbing her cold legs, trying not to cry. Flames danced to entertain her.

Then she returned to the window. Beneath the street lamp the road lay unmarked but for the yellow stain of electric light. In the garden, rhododendron leaves held handfuls of snow.

The moon peered in at the top corner of the window.

For long minutes she stood, heart bumping; but content. She had won the first round.

Then a car approached from the direction of the castle, and she remembered it was still evening; that Mother and Father were busy downstairs.

The car rolled slowly over the snow. She saw the familiar front of a Mercedes.

The car slid beneath the lamp post and stopped opposite the drive entrance. Behind the car window a face turned, looking.

The window descended.

In the moonlight Marion saw a young forehead above shadows which hid a movement of eyes.

Anger stirred in Marion. *If he has my gift,* she thought, *he must use it responsibly!* And she rushed in her mind, close to the car window, and mentally shrieked.

The boy's cry rose to her in the bedroom. The face ducked, and the car spun out of sight, its headlights lancing towards the village.

"Looking for a place to turn!" whispered Marion fiercely. "I dare you to go home! I dare you to retrace your journey past my gate! You think to use fear against me! It is your fear that sends the imps into the moonlight. It is your fear that dwells in darkness! Beware the light! Beware the light!"

"Marion!" Derek's voice. "Who are you talking to?"

"Myself!"

She stared over the polished water of the loch.

She breathed deeply, then realized she had told a lie.

She had said "Myself!" to protect Derek. Father was right. Love was more important than Truth.

She went and sat on the floor, her feet at the fire, her back against the bed. Derek's hand found her hair, patted.

"I'm warm," he said.

Marion nodded against his palm, smiling. She had no sense of the Mercedes returning. The room really was warm.

THURSDAY MORNING

They rose to a crisp white world. The sky

50

stood blue behind the mountains. Ferns of frost thickened the window. The snow pad on the window-sill, Marion saw with relief, really was unbroken. She grinned, and raced Derek to the bathroom, letting him win, washing herself at the washhand basin, shivering by the fire's cold ashes; dressing in woolly tights, cord trousers and ankle-warming boots. She bounced into a baggy jumper, and was brushing her hair when Derek raced in and buried himself back in bed.

"Be dressed," warned Marion, "by the time I come back!" But Father was in the bathroom, lathering his jaws, his slim arms exposed to the cold. "You could do that in your bedroom!" wailed Marion dancing on one foot. "You've got a washhand basin!"

"I forgot," said Father. "Won't be long. Use the loo downstairs," he suggested, and she fled to the toilet under the stairs.

She was washing her hands when a red blur moved past the window, wheels pressing through snow. She dried her fingers on the cold towel, ran across the hall, along the passage, through the kitchen – which was less freezing than the rest of the house, into the utility room – which was surprisingly warm considering the gap beneath the outside door. Marion noticed the central heating boiler; and envelopes on the floor.

She unbolted the door and said, "Hello!" as

the postman sat again in his van.

"Hello."

"I'm Marion."

"Ah!" The postman untangled himself from behind the steering wheel and stood in his boots on the snow. He towered, taller than Father, heavy, white hair brushed flat above a kindly face. "Good morning," he said, in a fine Scots drone. "I'm George."

Marion beamed. Instantly, she loved this man.

He smiled back. "Are you settling in?"

"Yes, thank you. Can you stay? I hear Mother in the kitchen. A cup of tea! Please stay. You have to meet everyone."

"That's very kind."

"Come on then!"

She led George inside, and shuffled the letters onto the table. "Father made the table," said Marion. "Mother. This is George."

"Mrs Kent," said George.

Father and Derek approached along the passage, Father trying to explain why it was impossible to fly at light speed.

"Oh," said Father. "You must be George."

"Good morning, Professor Kent."

"This is Derek. I think he's going to be a mathematician. Light years!" he groaned. "Before breakfast. At least I don't have to start at the University for a few days. Sit down." Father glanced at the letters. "Electricity

Board. Can't be a bill, yet. And two circulars. Something for Miss Kent. No stamp or postmark." He slipped the envelope to Marion. "Can I help, Lizzie?"

"Kettle's nearly boiling," said Mother.

"I only brought three," said George.

"Could you take a slice of bacon?" smiled Mother.

"Thank you. No. A cup of tea will warm me up. I don't think I've recovered from yesterday. Terrible thing, yesterday —"

"Sandy told us," said Derek.

"It must have been dreadful," agreed Mother. "The old man sitting on the doorstep."

"Cold as stone," nodded George.

Marion lifted the white envelope, and George's gaze, mild and surprised, watched her fingers as she picked the flap. She pulled a card out onto Father's table.

"Thank you," said George, as Father poured tea. "Delivered by hand."

"What have y'got?" asked Father. "An invitation?"

"Someone was up early," said George. "Or perhaps late last night. I don't recognize the writing." His large head angled at the envelope.

"That's a Beardsley," remarked Father staring at the card. "Tea for Derek?"

"Milk," said Derek. "Please. What's a Beardsie?"

"An artist," said Father. "1890s. Beardsley."

"Beards-ley."

"That's it. Aubrey Beardsley."

"A lady?"

"Not Audrey. Aubrey. Lizzie, your son's getting deaf. Marion?"

The drawing decorating the card displeased Marion. Old-fashioned ladies and gentlemen posed in black, but their elegance, thought Marion, covered corruption. And their beautiful faces were used for hiding thoughts, not expressing them.

"It's from the castle, Dad." Marion let the card lie on the table. She knew the people in the Mercedes had taken up her challenge and returned – not only past her gate, but through it, to deliver this horrid drawing.

Father swept it away. "Lady Ferguson requests the Kent children – doesn't know your names... Oh. To a birthday party. Callum. Something. Who's Callum? Does Lady Ferguson have a son?" he asked George. "Or a grandson?"

George lifted the envelope.

Mother put bacon and tomato down, but Marion's stomach closed up.

"Lady Ferguson," said George frowning at the envelope, "has no relations now. Except a son-in-law who doesn't live here. She keeps herself to herself."

"When are we going?" asked Derek, and Marion stared in surprise. Then she remembered that he knew almost nothing.

"I don't suppose it's everyone who is invited," said Mother, serving Derek with sudden dignity.

"I'm sure you're right, Lizzie," said Father gently, his dark gaze watching Marion. She shrugged a tiny shrug, as if to say, "We can't discuss it now." And Father said, "Well, it's more than a week away."

George's head shook slowly, then firmly. He pressed the envelope onto the table. "That's not Mary Ferguson's handwriting."

"I don't suppose she writes her own invitations," murmured Mother, as if serving breakfast was a hobby and servants lingered in the passage.

"Why should she write it at all?" asked Father, his eyes still on Marion. "Why should Lady Ferguson write invitations to Callum's party, if Callum is the boy genius who lives in the other portion of the castle? It's not her party."

George's gentle mouth turned down.

Mother tilted her head as if she knew the answer, but chose to stay silent.

Derek ate.

Marion said, "To make it seem safe."

8

*Derek and Marion discover monsters all
around; and something crawling
in Sandy's house*

The children walked, lunch warm in their
stomachs, anorak hoods down to let the sound
of the loch, the silence of the mountains touch
their ears; to let their heads turn freely, seeing
the sparkling landscape, the red and white
ferries crossing one another on the distant
estuary.

"It's so beautiful!" said Marion. "I can't
believe it's so beautiful!"

"The logs were beautiful," said Derek, and
Marion remembered the tree pieces cut by
Father.

"Yes. They were," she agreed.

"When we stacked them in a row at the side
of the house. Forty-three —"

"You counted them!" laughed Marion.

"The biggest one came up to here," said Derek patting his chest. "They turned into a diplodocus. Or a triceratops. A triceratops. It had little branches for horns and a scaly back. We have a prehistoric monster in our garden."

"And all around," said Marion. "Rocky monsters on the beach drinking at the loch. And the mountains are monsters, asleep for a thousand million years!"

Derek shouted. "Years!" so that their two voices sped across the water and eider-ducks bustled among boulders muttering, "Ooh? Ooh?" sounding so surprised that the children laughed.

They walked on, Marion's feet secure in wellingtons, a yellow carrier jumping at her wrist, Derek's cheeks fat, and pink with cold.

"Can you remember what we've to buy?" asked Marion. "I can't believe this place is so beautiful!"

"Eight things. Milk. . ."

"Get them in order."

"Eggs. . ."

"Right."

"Milk. Smash. Firelighters. . ."

"Good."

"Matches. Tomato soup. *The Glasgow Herald*. Salt for the steps."

"Now backwards."

"Oh."

"Use Father's trick."

Derek stopped and closed his eyes.

Someone on the beach clambered among the monsters, gathering driftwood. The figure straightened and waved, dropping wood. She shrugged with both palms, laughing, her voice trickling over the snow.

"It's Sandy."

"Salt. *Herald*. Soup. Matches. Firelighters. Smash. Milk. Eggs. Where?"

They waved. "Well done," said Marion.

"Your turn."

So Marion pictured the items in a pile, one on top of the other, and said the list forwards and backwards in almost one breath.

"Hello, there!" rose from the beach, and Sandy, hands in multicoloured knitted mittens, clutching a slipping bundle of wood, approached the raised grass verge. She heaved the wood onto a dark square on the grass.

"Let's see if she's still scared," said Marion. "And keep your mouth shut," she added cheerfully as they crossed the snow-churned road.

Sandy disappeared below the level of the grass. She popped up heaving another bundle on top of the first.

"Hello," said Marion. The dark square was a piece of carpet, canvas side up, blue rope knotted through holes at the edges.

"I say," cried Sandy. "Lean on this heap you chaps." And she ducked again and launched a log, thick as your thigh, up from the beach, denting the snowy grass. She rolled it with mittened palms, onto the carpet. "Catch the rope! Pull it together!" She leapt up and her hands flickered, snatching ropes from Derek — then from Marion as she hesitated — and knots appeared, knots that slid tight, drawing the carpet around the bundle, choking the sticks, throttling the log.

"Want to give it a pull? You in a hurry? Come and meet Mungo."

"We're only going to the shop," said Derek.

"Grab a rope then. Heave, ho!"

So they grabbed ropes and heave-hoed homewards for a hundred paces, but instead of dragging the carpetful of wood over their own footprints into their new home, they dragged it up the nearer drive, next door. Their feet found pebbles under the snow.

Then they stopped behind Sandy's house at stables large enough for just two horses.

Beside the stables dozed a monster of chopped logs, with a plastic sheet over its shoulder, to keep off the snow.

"We put ours indoors to dry," said Derek.

"I know," said Sandy. "Helped your dad, didn't I? But they should be outside. Like those. I didn't like to say."

"Some are outside."

"Just the little ones go inside." Sandy opened the stable door and encouraged her helpers with manly gestures and an authoritative, "Whoa!" Then she released the knots in the blue rope, and three pairs of hands clattered the wood into a corner.

"The smaller sticks are for kindling," explained Sandy. "They'll dry in here. The logs go outside. If they dry too much, they burn away in a jiffy. And if they're too wet with water or sap, they smoke and spark or won't catch. Best let them weather a year. Then — wow! The scent of burning wood! Very countrified to you kids, eh? But it's the way to live! You hungry?"

"We've just had lunch," said Marion.

"Ah. But are you hungry?" Sandy smiled her half smile and peeled off her woolly fingers in a business-like way. "Little Derek's nodding, I see."

"He's greedy."

"So will you be, my girl. Nodding, I mean. Come on. Hold it a sec."

She hoisted the carpet against the barn wall looping the rope around wooden pegs. "For harness originally," she said patting a peg. "Hasn't been a horse here in fifty years. That'll let the carpet dry. Derek! Forward! Left, right. Off we go! In the back door. There's a snowflake. Best place for flotsam is just where you saw me on the beach. Opposite the house there's never anything."

"What's flotsam?"

"Things washed up on the shore," said Marion.

The kitchen was hot and smelt of baking. Worktops lay clean, with storage jars pushed to the back. A food mixer stood tilted, its dough-hook softly spiked with brownish dough.

"Bread," said Sandy. "It's in the oven. Time it was out. Stand back, men." She spread her hands into oven gloves and whisked four loaf tins, swollen with hot bread, onto a grid. "OK. Let's get the kettle on. Marion, could you do that while I doff the wellies? Derek. See that square tin? Haul the lid off, there's a good chap. You'll find a plate in that cupboard."

"Fruit slice!" said Derek.

"Fly cemeteries," confirmed Sandy, sending her bent smile to Marion.

"Your kitchen's marvellous!" said Marion. "You must do a lot of cooking."

"Quite a bit. Of baking. There's only the two of us, mind, but George eats a lot —"

"The postman lives here?" cried Derek.

"No! Ha! Ha! He drops in when he's finished his rounds. Between you and me, I don't think his wife's too hot in the kitchen. And he likes his grub, does old George. No. My main outlets are the hotels —"

"You sell your baking!"

"Oh, yes. And coffee shops. I do my rounds too. As well as George, I mean. Three or four times a week. Everything from soup to ice-cream – got a new order this morning for the castle. That shook me! Hasn't been a do there in donkey's years –"

"You make ice-cream!" whispered Derek. "Mother can't do that."

"Just as well," said Marion, poking his tummy, but her mind hung on Sandy providing food for the castle. "Is the castle's order for next week?" she asked.

"That's right. How d'you know?"

"We've been invited. It's Callum's birthday. Oh, Derek! You're not supposed to start eating until you're asked!"

"Cups here," said Sandy, and she winked at Derek and Derek glanced at Marion through a blush. Marion grinned, and helped set dishes on the table.

"Is Mungo your boyfriend?" asked Derek.

"Ha! If you like!" grinned Sandy. "Let's find him!" And Marion smiled, guessing that Mungo was a cat.

She followed Sandy into a hall, lit only by daylight slipping through the glass of the front door. The carpet smelled of dust, and a black sideboard rough with carving, bore the sort of junk most people store in the attic, including, saw Marion, books in foreign languages.

An elephant startled Marion. It stood in the shadow of the sideboard, large as a barrel. Marion reached to pat its head but its wooden trunk was crinkled into a sneer. She turned away. An oil painting, mountainous with water, seemed real enough to fall into.

Marion's heart beat too fast. She looked around, searching for a cat-shape, but saw nothing except more paintings, and curtains swaggered back from a stair window, their folds, even in this light, pale with dust.

"Mungo!" whispered Sandy. "Ch! Ch! Mungo? Mummy's here. He's around somewhere."

Marion found Derek beside her, making crumbs with his fly cemetery; and they both smiled at Sandy calling herself "Mummy".

They wandered after Sandy into a room bulked with darkness. Threads of daylight stretched from shut curtains to spots on the walls.

"The curtains keep the heat in," explained Sandy. "Mother —"

She stopped, her hand whispering on wallpaper. A switch clicked, and light, gloomier than the darkness, swamped the room, displaying ancient furniture and, above the fireplace, a great mirror set in a gold frame.

And in the mirror, movement.

Sandy gasped.

Marion cried, "Oh!"

"What is it?" complained Derek.

A settee, with its back towards them, had something crawling along its arm.

9

Sandy's mother praises the cat,
and Sandy mentions a letter

Nightmares had filled Marion's nights when she was small.

Nightmares had filled her days too, when her gift was a burden no one knew existed, and she was too young to understand: finding herself, without effort, in a strange street or bewildered in someone's living room, or once, screaming among chimneys on a roof high above the city.

And nightmare was on her again.

She snatched at Derek's wrist, heart surging, and made an adrenalin-quick twist to the door –

Sandy swore – finishing with an "Oh!" of relief, making Marion hesitate; giving her confidence to face the settee; and she gasped to still the beating in her chest.

"You made me drop my cake!" said Derek.

"Oh!" yelled Marion.

On the arm of the settee lay a hand.

Above the settee's back, grey hair bobbed, and a voice, tight with age and anger demanded to know who had switched on the light.

"Mother!" sighed Sandy. "Who do you think switched on the light? Why are you sitting here in the dark?"

"I'll sit where I like in my own house! Who's this?"

The woman, standing up, glowered at Marion and Derek, then the glower changed to a simpering smile, and her hands preened pigtails and continued downward, pressing the front of her dressing-gown, posing with her feet in a man's slippers. "How do you do?" she pronounced.

"How do you do," breathed Marion.

"This is Marion, Mother. And Derek. Professor Kent's children. I told you the professor used the phone yesterday –"

"Oh! Professor Kent's children! How delightful! Has Sandy offered you a drink? He doesn't always remember his manners. Sandy! How could you!"

"Upstairs, Mother," said Sandy gently. She held her mother's arm, and raised a regretful eyebrow at Marion. "She loses the place sometimes."

"Sometimes," agreed the woman. "You

wouldn't think I was eighty."

"Mother, if you were eighty I would be forty. Come along. I'll bring you a nice cup of tea and a fly cemetery."

Marion backed into the hall with Derek, allowing Sandy to ease her mother towards the stairs. On the stairs, beneath the swag of curtain, two eyes shone yellow.

"There's a cat," said Derek. "Is that Mungo?"

"Oh, Mungo!" The woman's hand gestured towards the cat. "A wonderful mouser. Useful, useful creature! I quite adore him," she said as Sandy encouraged her up the stairs. But Sandy's furry head shook and the cat cringed, then raced down skidding on the hall parquet, gripping the carpet and hurtling towards the kitchen.

"Boil the kettle again," said Sandy to Marion. "Won't be long. Mother, why do you pretend? You know you can't stand the cat. . . You'd impress people more if you put your clothes on. . ."

Marion and Derek gaped at each other as the voices ascended through shadows. Then Derek dived into the room with the mirror, and Marion was just able to prevent the cake, dust and all, from entering his mouth.

"Hog!" she whispered, and dragged him to the kitchen. "Sit there and don't move. Why don't you count something!"

Derek's gaze followed the cake's descent into a pedal bin, and Marion gave him a dangerous look.

"She called Sandy 'him'," said Derek. "Doesn't she know?"

"She's confused. Old people get confused."

"Why?"

"Because they're old. I don't know why. I wonder where the tea is."

"The cat's in its basket."

"Oh!"

Marion forgot tea, and spoke to the cat until it offered a whiskered cheek. She rubbed the cheek, then found Mungo's skull with her fingertips. The cat's eyes reduced themselves to slits of ecstasy.

Sandy came in. "Good as gold, this boy," she said, touching Derek's head.

"He's been well warned," said Marion. "I had to put a piece of your cake in the bin. He dropped it."

"She knocked it out of my hand!"

"He would have eaten it off the floor!"

"Ha! Don't worry. Tea. Lapsang Souchong? Young Hyson? Fou-chow-foo? Scented Orange?" She smiled at one side of her mouth. "Lemonade?"

"Yes!" said Derek.

"Yes, please," agreed Marion. "Do you really have all those teas?"

"Oh, yes." Sandy leaned towards her guests

to tell them a secret. "Plus Typhoo and Tetley tea bags, for those who can't tell the difference." Marion smiled, suddenly realizing she liked this strange person; that the manliness was a protection, and beneath lived a woman working out the pattern of her life.

"I have a cat collection," said Marion.

"You can add Mungo, from the look of it," laughed Sandy, as the cat rolled to its feet and followed Marion's fingers. "Take your jackets off, chaps. OK. Lemonade. Fruit cake. What sort of cat collection?"

"Oh. Ceramic cats –"

"Brass cats," supplied Derek, then stopped his mouth with cake.

"A glass cat from Limerick."

"Where you saw —"

"Hush!"

Sandy poured tea into a thin cup, tasting it, not spoiling it with milk or sugar. "What did you see?" She coughed as if to destroy her question before it reached Marion's ears.

"She saw a flood."

"Will you shut up!"

"If you don't want to tell me. . ." And from the flicker of Sandy's eyes, Marion thought she should talk of something else.

But Sandy laughed her single, "Ha!" shielding her glance with her eyelids, intent on the turning surface of her tea. "Can't keep secrets around here, y'know. Best t'tell and get it accurate. Spit it out, old thing. Somebody likes the fly cemeteries —"

"Oh, Derek! Stop! You're so rude!"

"Ah, don't worry. A compliment to my baking. My mother sees things."

Marion stopped with her teeth half sunk in pastry. She completed the bite, startled at the block of silence that occupied the kitchen. *She* had seen things. Imps in the snow.

"She'd tell you there are pixies among the raspberries," blurted Sandy, "and ghosts in the Plantation — that's the trees behind your hothouse. Ha! And she's not eighty. Sixty-six and nutty as a string of conkers. My father ran away when I was little. I think he wanted a boy. Mother never was... You know. Bit emotional... You heard her. Says, 'my own house' every chance. That's because I maintain it. She hasn't a bean. I pay the lot with my baking. Wow! Didn't mean to spill all that! You're supposed t'be telling me!"

Sandy sat back folding her arms. "C'mon. What about this flood of yours? You know. . ." She relaxed, drooping in the chair.

Her pale blue eyes were defenceless, and her slight smile quite natural to a girl's lips. "Mother's worse. Since the autumn. Since the leaves began to fall. A breeze rattled through all the gardens.

"I was on the beach, with an armful of sticks. There was something about the way the

70

wind gathered strength. So deliberate. And with a chill to it that could draw the life out of you. Birds rose off the rocks and flew fast. And something I'd never seen before. The loch boiled. That's what I thought at first. A great patch of water, churning. But it was fish. As if they were panicking. And when I came in to the house, Mother was gaga. Weeping. She didn't know why. Or wouldn't explain. I had extra orders to make up. Meringues and scones. It was a holiday weekend and the coffee shops were busy. And a birthday cake for Agnes Lampton's girl. I'm afraid I didn't have much patience. I didn't realize it was serious. She'd been tidying the front garden. Poor Mother. George popped in and chatted to her. Which is more than I do, I suppose. They've known each other since they were kids, though Mother considers George a bit beneath her. According to George, it was the very day that Callum and the German moved into the castle.

"Mother sat in the hall for a week afterwards, staring, saying the elephant would move if she took her eyes off it. Huh." Sandy's mouth bent upwards; but she stared at Marion. "Silly old fool."

"What is it?" breathed Marion. "Is there something else?"

"Driving me as daft as herself. I always thought the elephant's trunk came straight

71

back along its flank. But it's bent into a sneer. At least it is now. That's why I scarpered out of your kitchen yesterday. I don't like spooky talk. It could be true," she whispered.

10

*Marion follows a sigh,
and Sandy remembers*

Sandy hurried to the loaves on the worktop and emptied them from their tins onto the grid.

"Your mother may be sensitive," said Marion.

"Haw!" squawked Sandy, but her eyes slid doubtfully. "I mean," she said, "it's nonsense. Who says there's anything to be sensitive about? Who says there's anything wrong at the castle? Sometimes birds leave an area. And fish too, probably. Means nothing. Take my word for it, young Marion. . ."

Marion knew her gaze was crumbling Sandy's false confidence.

Then Marion's mind shifted.

Tall shadows stood around the staircase. Daylight seeped in the window behind the dust-draped curtains.

A sigh took Marion into a bedroom.

Curtains here, shut out winter's cold, and a lamp dropped light on Sandy's mother as she rocked in a chair. She hugged something, and moaned as if nursing a sick baby.

Then the woman's pigtails swung and her face blackened with shadow as she stared around the room.

"Sandy? I know you're there! Stop playing silly games with Mummy! Why don't you wear a dress like other little girls? You mustn't blame Daddy. He needed a boy to help with his miracles. Sandy? Where are you? I won't have that cat laughing at me again!"

She stood up, and dropped the object she'd been hugging. It was one of her very large slippers. She put her foot into it.

"Kindly –" she quavered, "– do not follow me to the lavatory."

"Marion?" said Sandy.

"Marion!" Derek was pulling her fingers. She opened her eyes to the colours of the kitchen.

"You gave us a turn, old thing! Off in a dream world. . ."

"Your mother's gone to the toilet," breathed Marion. "She knew I was there. She really is sensitive."

As Marion spoke, Sandy's face paled under the dry skin, and she retreated horrified into her chair.

"It's all right!" said Derek. "I hate it too.

74

But she can't help it."

"Can't help it?"

"It's not a disease," said Marion. "It's a gift. Everyone has a gift —"

"Father says —"

"Some people dance, or bake." Marion smiled encouragingly. She didn't want Sandy frightened. "I can project myself into other places. But I'm not nosy. That would be awful! I use it carefully, you know. When I feel I should. When I feel someone should be convinced. Like you."

"Me?" gasped Sandy. She stood up, her eyes large and blue in her white face. She bustled with the kettle, rinsing her cup, selecting a strong Typhoo. "Why should I have to know?"

"But you asked," said Derek.

"Be quiet!" hissed Marion.

"I did ask, but. . ."

"I don't know why," said Marion, glaring at Derek, "but sometimes it's important for a person to know. I go by my feelings. The only person I told in Limerick about the cracked water-main under the road turned out to be an engineer."

She smiled.

"Ha!" said Sandy. "I've got shortbread. Broken pieces I can't sell. This tin, I think."

"Your mother thought I was you, spying on her."

"She would." Sandy sat down with fresh tea. "It's her latest fad. Silly old goat."

"Don't you like your mother?" said Derek. "May I have more lemonade please?"

"Ha! Ha!" laughed Sandy. "Help yourself! Like her? Well. How can you like someone who never makes sense? But I love her." Sandy gulped her tea.

She trembled her cup onto its saucer. "She's angry with God because my father left her. When I was five. Tall, skinny man, I remember, with a funny way of talking. Then *he* became her god. Though he overate. For energy. So she said. But he would live for ever! According to her. Huh! Then she stopped mentioning him. I think she realized she was talking too much nonsense to a child. She turned it inwards. Probably that's why she's a bit screwy now."

She stared at Marion. "Wow," she said. "I shouldn't be telling a couple of kids."

"Father says," announced Derek through a fistful of shortbread, "that everyone confesses to Marion. She should be a priest —"

"Oh be quiet!"

"— or a policeman. But I don't know what that means."

"It means you're always blabbing," said Marion cruelly; and she continued. "I think he's insecure because he's quite a lot younger than me, and can't do what I do. That's why he eats so much —"

"I don't!"

"How many cakes have you had? Suddenly he can't count."

"I think he's crying."

"Oh!" said Marion. "I'm sorry! I don't mean to be cruel! I want to be the kindest person who ever lived. But he's so annoying! We'd better go before he's sick. Eating and crying are sure to bring it on. I'm not getting at you now!" she shouted, as Derek sobbed. "Anorak! What were we to buy? How many things?"

"Eight things!" gasped Derek.

"Show Sandy your good memory."

"Smash. Firelighters. Matches. Soup. *Herald*, salt, eggs, milk!"

"Well done. You started in the wrong place but they were in the right order."

"I can sing too," Derek told Sandy. "I sing when Father plays the piano. Shall I sing you something?"

"No!" said Marion, hauling his anorak up his arms. "Say, 'thank you' to Sandy."

So they thanked Sandy, and left her preparing a tray for her mother.

11

*Marion is anxious
and Derek throws snowballs*

Snow had gathered, thicker than ever, on the timbers of Sandy's stable and in the forks of trees.

The children stood on the pavement, listening. Marion glimpsed the beach through the tumbling flakes.

"Can you hear the water?" she asked.

"No. I can see our gatepost."

"We have to get the shopping. Come on. We're terribly late already."

"Is it far?" Derek's hand searched down her arm and clutched her fingers.

"Not too far." Marion wished she had worn gloves. The yellow carrier hung on her wrist, heavy with a loaf still warm from Sandy's oven.

Silence dropped steadily around the children, and Marion wondered at Derek clinging to her instead of packing snow into snowballs. She wondered at herself, tense in the silence, stepping along, loaf nuzzling her thigh, lengthening the pavement between herself and home; keenly striding, little Derek hastening, fastened to her hand; white aprons solid on their fronts. And the water of the loch lying beyond their sight, its wet skin consuming a thousand million gems of crystal.

"You're going too fast."

"Try to keep up."

"Why are you hurrying? I don't want to hurry!"

"Do you want to be left alone?"

The silence pressed around them. Only the bag rustled, and snow creaked under their boots.

"I want to throw a snowball." But Derek's fingers didn't slacken their grasp.

Garden walls moved past. Hedges bristled at Marion over the walls. Laurel leaves stood green and white, and trees behind in the gardens waited until she was past.

"I can hear the water," said Derek.

"The shore's closer to the road here. It's not far to the shops now."

Something square hung from a branch.

"There's a notice," said Derek.

"Oh. It must be the hotel. The lettering's half-covered in snow. Can you read it?"

Derek read it.

"Not *Lock*view," said Marion. "Lochview Hotel. The shops are round the next bend. I think. I can hardly see anything. Good thing there's just the one road. We can't get lost."

"There are little roads going up the hillside."

"But we can't mistake them for the shore road. Isn't it cold! We should've had tea instead of lemonade. The telephone men will never get over the hill." Marion remembered the blue cable dangling on the house wall, and the vague anxiety which had been growing in her, became real.

"You're walking too fast!"

She slowed. For a moment she thought of leaving Derek under the hotel sign; but that was foolish, and she clenched her fingers around his hand and scudded on, snow leaping from her toes, Derek running and whining.

She shuddered, and the anxiety sharpened. Her mind sped away in a sweeping circle, instantly returning. She had felt no danger. But her feet took her into a gateway, Derek staggering, and she looked back.

Their footprints faded behind them. Beyond the footprints, she knew, was home, with Mother, dusting, or unpacking, Father making coffee, or setting fires; and beyond home, high on a rock, the castle, like a cliff gathering snow on its stonework, and within its walls, Lady Ferguson, and an emptiness as cold as the void of space.

"You *saw* something!"

"I see the shops," said Marion, and the wall disappeared beside her, and a space lay open, with a car or two, and footprints, and a pillar box, blood-red beneath its snowy cap. The shop windows shone warmly into the rushing weather.

Marion's anxiety melted in the shop's warmth. They chose their groceries, treating themselves – despite being full of Sandy's cakes – to a Mars bar each; reading notices about prams for sale, yachts for hire, talks in the library.

They went into the snow.

The cold gripped them. The yellow bag bumped heavily against Marion's knee.

"I can't hold your hand," she told Derek. "I'm eating my Mars bar." Derek stuffed the end of his chocolate into his mouth and crumpled the paper. "Put that in your pocket." He clung to her elbow. "At least it's not drifting into our faces," said Marion. "Isn't it thick!" And she smiled down on Derek, and he beamed fatly, crouching suddenly and squashing snow into a ball. He threw it across the road where it dug a little grave for itself in the white ground.

"Oh, terribly good," said Marion. "See if you can hit that lamp post." But the lamp post dodged, and snowballs made shadows in the road.

"You're hopeless!" cried Marion. She dumped the carrier and gripping her Mars bar in her teeth, threw a snowball, which nicked the lamp post, and exploded through the dropping air.

"You nearly missed!" yelled Derek.

Marion laughed, and Derek grabbed her arm, and swung half-angry.

Deep in Marion's mind her anxiety sighed, but so slight was it, that she crushed it with laughter and bounced Derek off the snow until his anger was gone and he didn't mind her skill at throwing. Then he ran ahead and ambushed her from behind a stone gatepost, bursting a snowball on the yellow carrier, another on her shoulder, sparking snow on her face.

She ate the last of her Mars bar, and dried her brow with her palm.

The anxiety swelled in her, and she sent her mind leaping forward, and found, beyond the next bend, the creeping shape of the black Mercedes.

12

*Marion plays a serious game,
and the ground trembles*

She rushed at Derek.

Derek gaped, a snowball balanced in his hand.

"Hide!" she cried.

"What for?"

"Behind the gatepost! Quickly!" She swept him into the unfamiliar driveway, pushing him and herself between the stone pillar and the rigid fingers of a hawthorn.

She dropped the carrier, and caught Derek's face between her palms. His eyes stretched wide, and yellow hair clung to his forehead. She shifted her left hand onto his brow and swamped his mind with hers. His eyelids slid shut.

"A stone wall," he breathed.

"That's right," whispered Marion. "Pretend you are a stone wall." And she held him with

her hands and her thoughts, imagining herself
and Derek part of the stones that guarded the
gardens; stilling his mind, blocking the
probing darkness that crept around them as
the car sighed past beyond the gatepost.

Marion relaxed, and left Derek, motionless;
she trod in her own footprints, and saw a
winking light as the car turned into the open
space at the shops. The rushing snow wiped
away the lamp post. Were they searching, that
man and the boy, for Marion? Or simply
buying groceries, and mind-searching out of
habit?

She wondered if she could rush Derek home
before the car came back. Her mouth twisted
as she made her decision. She returned to
Derek. "Come. Hurry." And he ran obedi-
ently, holding her hand, his mouth closed.

The bag struck Marion's knee painfully. She
looked back and saw blind falling snow.
Derek's mouth opened, gasping.

They ran, breaking snow with their feet;
clumsy evidence of their passing.

"Why are we running?" panted Derek. "It's
not a game?"

Air slid cold into Marion's mouth. "It's a
game!" she gasped. "But it's very serious. A
very serious game. Come on! Plod! Plod! Plod!
There's the hotel sign! Guess how many steps
till we're under it."

"Twenty!"

"One! Two! Three! Ow! Four!" They slowed, legs aching, throats chilled.

"Ah!" cried Marion, and she stopped under the sign. "Forty-one? I'm puffed!"

"It looked like twenty!"

"Without the snow it might have been twenty." Marion flickered her mind back seeking the car, and headlights rolled at her. "Time to hide again!" She ran Derek the few paces to the hotel driveway, and they crouched behind the wall. "This time," she said brightly, "we'll be. . . ?"

"Bushes!"

"Bushes. Bushes it is!" And she reached to him with her hands, drowning him in thoughts cold and green. His eyes closed, and his panting eased. Silence sat in their heads, until it seemed that any passer-by glancing over the wall would see, not two children crouching in a game, but two bushes, unheeding beneath the endless snowflakes.

Through her stillness Marion heard the hiss of tyres, the purr of power as the Mercedes moved at the other side of the wall. It passed the drive entrance. Another mind, alighted on hers like a questioning bird, then flitted away. The sound faded.

Around her, the snow thickened the ground, turning the landscape into a great iced cake.

She stood up slowly.

Tyre tracks ran into the white daylight, and Marion breathed with relief. Her face tingled in the cold air. "Come on, Snow Boy," she said. "We must get home. Mother will be worrying. Unless Sandy thought to pop through."

"Is the game over? My face is as cold as a real snow boy. Is there anything to eat in the bag?"

"You've just had a Mars bar! And you know there isn't."

They walked, Derek lifting snow from a wall, but in the shrouding weather found no target, and lobbed the snowball high, losing it until it plopped softly at Marion's foot.

The tyre tracks, already whitening, led Marion homeward. Derek walked close, counting steps, taking her hand, springing snow from twigs, singing. Marion's mouth tasted of chocolate. The tyre pattern attracted her eye, and she let it ripple beside her, smoothing under the dashing flakes, flowing with every curve of the road, burrowing into the dazzling air, tramp! in the snow went her wellingtons. "Dee!" sang Derek, and released her hand. "Dee, dee!" he trilled behind her. Tramp! in the snow, tyre tracks in her eye taking her onwards tramp! dee! in the distance, tramp! tramp! Tracks flowing, swift on the road, filling her vision, Marion striding, nothing behind her, stepping along, Marion's breath out and in, the tug of the bag dragging her arm, nudging her knee —

Pain in her knee. She drew in her breath in a groan. "Oh, this bag!" She changed the bag to her other hand. "Surely we should be home?"

She turned. "Derek!" she said. "Derek!"

A sound.

"Derek?"

Suddenly snowflakes ceased their rushing, and floated gently. Trees appeared looking over walls. Houses shone yellow windows at her. The loch sighed.

Before her, a heavy *clunk*.

Under her jumper cold spread over her back. *Clunk*.

"Derek?" But she knew Derek was somewhere behind her. The tracks of the Mercedes were almost filled with snow. She breathed firmly through her nose, hesitating about sending her mind to search.

"Who's there?" she croaked.

Clunk.

She stepped backwards, peering. She jumped at the slither of snow from a branch.

Something moved.

The clunk vibrated the pavement even through its winter cushion.

Marion's mouth twisted. She could imagine nothing at all that would shake the ground as it walked. Was it a machine?

It came out of the snow, and tears blurred

her sight. She blinked fiercely, and wiped her eyes.

She moaned, turned her back, and ran as she had never run in all her life.

13

*Marion drinks brandy
and Father takes a stroll*

The bag fled from her fingers. Her feet beat
along the broken snow she had just trod. The
rim of her wellingtons bumped her shins. The
anorak hood interfered with her balance and
her hand leapt to throw it back.

She heard her name.

"Derek!" she screamed.

He was crouched in a gateway packing snow
into a mound. He called again, grinning. "We
went past the house —"

His face drooped with surprise as Marion
ran at him. She wrapped her arms around him,
lifted him and staggered up the drive, dumping
him, dragging him onward, making him run,
screaming, "Run! Run!" And he caught her
fear and galloped with her down the side of the
house, past the white-topped pineapples of the
clothes poles, Father's chopping block soft

with snow, crashing open the back door, throwing Derek into the utility room, slamming the door, fumbling desperately with the bolts, shoving them across, shutting out the horror, screaming until her mind turned blind inside her skull.

Voices and hands brought her out of it. Tight in Father's arms, she stumbled into the kitchen. She wept. Hot tea on her lips.

Then she pushed free of Father's grasp and dashed suddenly to the dining room, feeling the warm breath of the fire wafting from the black fireplace. She rushed to the window and looked down the drive.

Father, Mother and Derek gathered behind her.

"Marion?" said Mother.

Derek snuffled.

"Now," said Father lightly. But no one stirred, and dropping snowflakes pretended all was well. "You're trembling," said Father, his hand on Marion's shoulder. "You're not hurt. . ." It was half a question, and Marion shook her head.

"There's something out there." Her voice rattled on her breath.

"I don't see anything," said Father gently. "What was it? A man? A dog? You're not scared of dogs."

"Oh, Daddy!" Marion turned. A sob

surprised her.

"I think," murmured Father, "a stroll is demanded –"

"It was a dwarf," whimpered Marion.

"A dwarf!" cried Mother. "Really –"

"A dwarf!" screamed Marion. "A dwarf! A dwarf!"

"Marion!" said Father. "Did he touch you?"

"No! Oh, Daddy! He was wearing the most awful mask! Like those things on Notre Dame Cathedral –"

"A gargoyle?"

"Yes. And he was carrying something. On his back. A rucksack? It sat high up behind his head. But –"

She rocked nervously, remembering, trying not to remember. "Daddy." Father's serious eyes met hers. "Daddy!"

"What is it?"

"When he walked," she whimpered, "the ground shook."

Father's head tilted questioningly. Muscles in his cheek made one eye close slightly.

"It did!" whispered Marion.

"Well. Surely. . ." Father raised an eyebrow. "Surely a lorry somewhere. . ."

Marion's head moved from side to side. "No!" she breathed. "Clunk! and the pavement vibrated. Clunk!" she cried. "Clunk! Clunk! Every step! The ground shook!"

Derek wailed and clung to Mother. Mother stared at Marion, bewilderment in her round face. "John!"

"You take care of her, Lizzie. Another cup of tea perhaps. Even a sip of brandy. I won't be long."

"Daddy —"

But he left quickly.

She watched him hurry down the drive, new green wellingtons encasing his legs, a scarf knotted, ends dancing on his jumper, hands in pockets. He moved cheerfully, she thought. He vanished beyond the gatepost. Trees and evergreen shrubs, maturing through a hundred and fifty years, blocked her view. Only from upstairs could she see onto the road.

Mother pushed a cold glass into her hand and Marion sipped brandy. Three sips finished the brandy, but it warmed her.

Then Father reappeared round the gatepost swinging the yellow carrier. He lifted his face towards the window and smiled.

Marion ran to the kitchen. The kettle spread condensation on a cupboard door. "May I have coffee this time?" she asked Mother. Father passed the window. Sounds in the utility room as he removed his boots. In he came, hauling at the scarf's knot, placing the carrier on his table, disgorging the carrier. "Eight items," he murmured. "Nine?"

"Did you find anything?" asked Mother.

"No," said Father. "Salt. Milk. Smash. Firelighters. Matches. Soup. Eggs. *Herald*. A Mars bar wrapper? And a loaf?"

"We met Sandy," said Marion, "and helped her carry driftwood from the beach."

"She gave us fruit slice."

"That's why you were so long," said Mother. She placed coffee mugs on pads. "Oh, that looks lovely!" She lifted the loaf.

"Sandy made it," said Marion. "She bakes and cooks for a living. You must have found something?"

She stared at Father.

He stared back.

Mother and Derek waited.

"No," said Father.

"Footprints!"

"Oh! Yes. Footprints! Lots of footprints –"

"Lots?"

"Lots. Looked as if a herd of elephants had got out of a car and wandered all over the pavement. With shoes on."

"Oh."

Marion grasped her mug tightly, holding it until her hands burned.

"There weren't any cars," said Derek. "I would have counted."

"There was at least one," smiled Father. "Tracks all along the road."

Marion put extra sugar in her coffee. The

93

sweetness calmed her. "A car went past earlier –"

"We hid!"

"– but it would have been gone by the time –" She gulped more coffee. "– by the time I saw that thing."

"A dwarf isn't a thing," said Mother. "It's a person –"

"It?" said Father, and Mother's mouth puckered into a rosebud, but relaxed when Father smiled.

"Why don't we walk along the road?" said Father. His slim hand held Marion's fingers. "Just the two of us. Before it's dark, mm?" And his eyes, shadows of blue, beckoned her.

"All right," said Marion.

"John. . ."

"Won't be long." Father looked at Mother. "I want Marion reassured. Just let me pull on the new green wellies again. Rather smart, eh?" And Marion, still dressed for outside, walked with him.

The air stood brittle with cold. The snow had stopped, and across the loch, the sun peered through a hole in the sky, its glance turning the waters pink, turning the beach and road pink, leaving the hills beyond the water in white dead shadow.

Marion shivered. She pointed at the

snow-filled tracks of the Mercedes. "It was *them*," she said.

"From the castle?"

She clung to Father. "That was why we hid. Derek thought it was a game. I think they have something to do with Sandy's mother."

"Oh?" said Father. "What?"

"I'm not sure. But they are here, in the village, because of her. I'm not sure," she said again.

They trod the pavement churned by her flight. "The boy touched my mind as the car passed, but I was being a bush, and he left me. Perhaps."

The tyre tracks suddenly ran dark.

"See?" said Father. "Footprints, all around here. I take it this is the place?"

"Yes. I think so."

Father pointed back. "I found the carrier just there."

"The pavement shook, Daddy," whispered Marion.

"I can't say I understand," said Father. "Let's follow the footprints."

"The sun's going behind the hills."

"Just a little way. They may be spoiled by morning. See the tyre tracks? These are fresher than the ones the Mercedes left. And the car turned around in this driveway."

"They're the same," said Marion. "I looked at them all along the road. They seemed to hypnotize me. I never saw our entrance. The Mercedes came back here after I'd run away, then the boy trampled about; it looks as if he ran up and down this pavement. Up and down."

They walked round a bend.

The road ran straight, then wriggled like a worm past a rock as high as a bus.

On the rock, the castle windows shone pink, snow on the stonework.

The pink slid from the windows, leaving the great building bleak and dreadful.

"The sun," said Father. "It's gone behind the hills."

14

*Father jumps to a conclusion
and Marion refuses to be alone*

A cold pool of desolation rose around Marion. The mountains stood black as cardboard, and the sun's fingers clung to a turquoise rent in the sky. Her heart beat dumbly. She stood, seeing the promontory where Sandy fished; seeing the road writhing, cut by the Mercedes' tyres; seeing snow on the pavement, dark now with night, broken by a row of footprints, that curved beneath the belly of rock.

"We must go back," she said.

"Wait." Father crouched, reaching into the snow. "Pity we haven't Derek's scrimshaw. Hmn." He sat on his heels looking along the pavement. He stood, then walked away through the gloaming. He bent, his body a question mark. His arm reached down again. A street light blinked sleepily, opening its one eye, watching Father.

"Come back!" whispered Marion.

Father's face moved pale in the darkness. It vanished as he turned away, plodding, his arm dipping like an elephant's trunk, into the footprints.

Quite slowly he went round the rock and out of sight.

Marion felt as lonely as an explorer in the Arctic.

And as cold.

She tramped on the spot and looked around. Two birds beat steadily across the dull gleam of the loch. They flew closer, approaching the promontory.

Marion smiled, enjoying the beauty of the birds' flight; pleased that the birds lived.

They staggered suddenly and Marion stared. Wings hammered the air and *quack!* came across the water, *quack!* The leading duck splashed on the surface of the loch and flapped wildly. It lifted, and curved after its mate, which had struck for the loch's centre – black now in the shadow of the mountains – away from the promontory.

"It's like fishing in the bath," whispered Marion, remembering Sandy's words, "for all the living things you see."

She looked up at the castle. Lights were on. She walked in Father's footprints. The other footprints were deep scores, too filled with darkness to see into. Callum, she thought, did not run this far, but returned to the car – he didn't cover the dwarf's trail completely.

She was so cold.

Her shadow, cast by the lamp post, crept around her like a slinking dog. The rock hung cold at her face. A lane invited her steeply upwards beside the rock, while the road hurried on towards more street lights.

Blocking the lane, was a low railing that Father could have stepped over. He turned, and Marion saw the glint of his smile. The castle reared beside him, filling the sky. She stood close to him. The railing was really a low gate. The footprints and tyre tracks continued beyond the gate up the slope of the lane past a doorway, where light spread from an outside bulb on the castle wall.

Marion hadn't realized how dark the winter day had grown. She looked down the lane. The loch lay silver among hills of coal. The rent in the sky was dark blue. The sun had let go and fallen behind the world.

Father swung the ends of the scarf thickly around his neck. "You were right," he murmured. "It was the same car." Beyond the gate, the eyes of the Mercedes watched them coldly.

A small balustrade followed steps up to the door, and the door stood shut beneath a sandstone arch. Windows made of lead and glass shone dully, and at the foot of the steps, poised as if on guard, a statue waited.

Marion shrank against Father. Her heart beat, and the cold of this place crawled under her ribs. Really, she was looking at nothing strange, but as her eyes widened to the shadows beside the light, she saw the stone creature, and her flesh shuddered.

The head was as she remembered, though now mainly in darkness. Light stroked the massive beak, tipped the knobbled horns, outlined the flopping ears. On its back, rising higher than its head, almost as high as Marion's head, heavy stone wings dropped into blackness at its feet.

Marion's hand found Father's palm. Father's breath shook. He fluffed out a little laugh, and muttered, "No wonder you thought it —" Then Marion felt him stand very still.

She knew what he had meant to say. "No wonder," she whispered, "I thought it was carrying a rucksack."

"Huh!" said Father, rather loudly.

His voice rattled off the rising wall of the castle.

"Hush!" whispered Marion.

"Even the scientific mind gets influenced by its surroundings! Fancy!" Marion tugged his hand, and he followed her. "What a conclusion to jump to!"

They descended to the road. "Need training

100

shoes for a leap like that."

They walked under the belly of rock. "Is that you shaking, or your father?"

Something shrieked on the loch.

They trudged the length of a garden wall.

"Now," said Father, pausing, shivering, "that must be where George found the old chap on the doorstep."

They peered up a driveway.

Marion could see only the bulge of a conservatory and chimneys defying the cold.

"Pretty ghastly," murmured Father, "going round this in the dark and a corpse waiting for its mail."

"Father –"

"Hold on."

"I'm freezing!" moaned Marion.

"There's someone in there!"

Shrubbery hung tall on both sides of the driveway.

"Didn't he live alone?" asked Marion.

"Mm. Eating boiled eggs and complaining to the press. Shouldn't have thought eggs were good for a man with heart trouble. I'll just take a look."

"What!"

"I saw a light moving. Can't walk away. We may be new in the district, but good neighbours are good neighbours –"

"But he's dead."

"No one," explained Father sneaking up the

drive with Marion still attached to his hand, "should be in that house. You cut along home..." Marion glanced back. The loch gleamed between masses of shrubbery.

"No! You come."

"Give me ten minutes," murmured Father, and he moved on, but Marion clung to him.

The conservatory glittered like a vast fly's eye, the faceted glass, reflecting touches of light from a lamp post. The house huddled in a garden black with trees and pale with lawns. The castle towered close. Something tiny dropped near Marion.

"It's snowing," she told Father.

15

*Marion and her father become burglars,
and find a door which they desperately need to
open*

Father's head searched the ground. "Do you
see any footmarks?"

"No."

"Then the burglar must have gone in the
back. This way."

He took her past the conservatory, quietly in
the snow, bending low to be invisible to
anyone inside.

Behind the house, outbuildings of various
heights confused their eyes. Father led Marion
into the heart of them. It was very dark.

Father released Marion's hand.

"What are you doing?" she whispered.

"Feeling for the door. Ah. It's open. Could
you ask your heart to stop making such a din?
This way. Up two steps. No carpet. Softly in
the wellies, my girl. I think it's *my* old heart —"

"It's your mouth, Father," hissed Marion,

knowing he was talking because he was scared.

"Hold it. Have you any matches? No. This is the kitchen. Feel around. Find the cooker."

"The cooker!"

"No noise! Ow! Oh! My favourite shin."

"I've found the cooker," hissed Marion. "Now what?"

"I'm coming. Is it gas?"

Marion felt the rings, and found holes in the burners. "Yes. It's horribly greasy."

"Then there may be matches. Feel around, child, feel around."

Marion fingered the worktop cautiously, finding a puddle of something thin and sticky, then a dead hand which she hoped was sausages.

Matches rattled. "Hah!" whispered Father. Scrape! Flare! And Father beamed, ghastly by matchlight. Then the light moved aloft, searching, but Marion saw nothing except Father's thumbnail and the dazzle of flame.

"Couldn't we switch on the light?"

"He'd be out the front door—"

"It was a joke," whispered Marion. "Please, let's go! I don't like this!"

The matchlight shrank and Father shook it into darkness. He scraped again and fumbled the box into Marion's hand. "You light one," said Father. "See if there's a candle. . ."

Scrape. Two wobbling lights moved around the kitchen. Glass doors of cupboards doubled the flames. Father made a noise with a chair. A circle blinked white at Marion, and she snatched at it, finding a sliding switch, click! and a ray of torchlight drowned Father's match.

"Well done!" Father's hand took the torch. "Stay close!"

The beam bobbed around cupboards then found a door. Father opened the door. Marion clutched the tail of his jumper.

The light dodged along a passage. It glinted on the glass of paintings.

Marion tiptoed behind Father's protective strength.

"The conservatory," he whispered. "This way."

They followed the torch into a hall large enough for a ballroom. Vast elaborate doorframes loomed on every wall, and ancient furniture cringed from the torch's beam. A fireplace yawned enormously, and a tall man stood in a corner. The torch found his face. He said, "Dong," solemnly, and Marion drew in a breath of surprise.

"Half-past five," said Father faintly. "On-ward."

A sitting room smelling faintly of pipe tobacco.

Beyond the windows, shrubbery printed leaf patterns against a street light; and french windows in the side wall of the sitting room lay open to the conservatory, mingling earth smells with the tobacco.

Father hurriedly switched off the torch. He stood still, and Marion listened. Should she send her mind among the glass-black panes? Something bumped, and Father's hand gripped her wrist forcing her behind an armchair. His hand settled on top of her head and pushed her down. Pat, pat. Father became a shadow.

She glimpsed the torch, a dead glint in the darkness. Father soared past a mirror. She hoped the burglar wasn't violent. Another bump.

She thought it came from across the room.

Someone ran. A head bobbed between Marion and the yellow haze outside. Marion glimpsed movement at the door that led to the hall. Then light danced from the conservatory and Father charged past. Marion ran, then walked, feeling her way.

A crash and a shrill cry from the kitchen.

"Well *done!*" from Father. Then, "Oh!" Swearing. "Oh!"

Marion found the kitchen light switch and pressed it.

Father stood with one hand clasped to his forehead, the other searching for something to lean on.

A chair lay across the open back doorway. Among the chair legs, sheets of paper rocked in a breath of cold air. A rubber torch rolled on tiles at the touch of Father's foot.

"Daddy!"

"Head wound only," gasped Father. He eased up his palm to let her examine his brow.

"It's not cut."

Marion placed a healing palm on his forehead.

"Thanks," said Father. "I think it was your dwarf."

"That isn't funny!"

"Small personage. Young voice. What a thump! He threw his torch. I say..." He pointed at the papers on the floor.

"I'll pick them up," said Marion. "It's letters. Should we read them? Will you phone the police?"

"Let's have a look. Oh, my head. 'To the Editor.' Hum. Complaining about holiday-makers messing up the beach. Here's another. Dead birds on the road... These are all copies. 'Yours faithfully, J. Merchantman'."

"Did you put the chair across the door-way?" asked Marion.

"While you were finding the torch," sighed Father. "Why would a burglar steal copies of an old man's correspondence?"

"Callum," said Marion.

"Callum? The boy from the castle?"

"I saw him against the street light. I've seen him before. In the Mercedes..." She recalled rushing, shrieking with her mind at the boy's face. She would mention the imps later.

"So," said Father.

"Will you call the police?"

Father lifted the chair and sat on it. He shivered.

"Are you all right?"

"The old man's desk was in the conservatory. It's warm there. I want to read these letters, but I'm so cold. . ."

"Take them home," said Marion.

"That would be stealing, my pet."

"I'll light the gas. Heat us up –"

"No, no. I want to look at the desk anyway. Though we'd better not put lights on. I suppose we're the burglars now. . . Oooh!" he shuddered, then they returned to the conservatory and heat, and bright green leaves where the torch touched. "Ah!" That's better. See if there's something I can put round my shoulders."

Father sat at Jack Merchantman's desk and prodded into drawers with the light.

Marion was tempted to say she couldn't search in the dark, but when she glanced away from the torch, enough street-glow spread into the sitting room to show the shapes of furniture. A smear of natural light crept over the foliage around Father. Marion wished he was wearing something warmer than a jumper and scarf. Then she realized she wasn't specially cold, and sharing with her father would be a step towards becoming The Kindest Person in the World. She unzipped her anorak and put it round him. He said, "Thanks," and continued sliding the torchlight over the letters.

"Nothing in the desk," he murmured. "Feel better now. This one is a complaint about the castle. Hold on. And it's not a copy. Well. Dated the day before yesterday. The old boy must've been going to post it yesterday, but his heart solved all his problems —"

"What does it say?" Marion paced among the plants. She was uneasy.

"Just let me skim through. . ."

Marion went into the sitting room. She wished she had lifted Callum's torch from the kitchen floor. She worked her way round the furniture to the window.

The lawn was a ghostly sea, rolling motionless and pale. The shrubs that hid the drive raged without moving. Snowflakes pressed on the windows, and slid.

From the conservatory Marion caught a murmur of Tchaikovsky's Serenade in C Major. She wondered how long she and Father had been in the house. Mother might be anxious. Marion recalled the dong of the grandfather clock. She felt her way to the hall.

It was very cold.

She pulled her jumper sleeves over her hands

and stood close to the man in the corner, peering up at his face. Twenty to six. Just ten minutes.

She remembered the shrill cry from the kitchen as Callum had fallen over the chair. Clever old Father. But what a little brute to throw the torch! And what a nerve to actually burgle someone's house!

She decided to go to the kitchen and switch off the light in case anyone investigated.

The investigators investigated, she thought.

The staircase was a black slope up to darkness. She hurried across the hall. Light from the kitchen lay on the floor of the passage.

Something bumped.

Surely Callum wouldn't come –

A blood-thickening scrape, like stone on stone.

Marion put her chilled back against the passage wall. A picture behind her head wobbled, and she snatched to hold it silent.

Thud.

The floor trembled.

Thud.

Marion shrank inside her jumper. Her fingers gathered up the woollen ends of her sleeves, and she shut her eyes.

Thud.

The floor vibrated against the soles of her

feet. She ran, wellingtons squealing on wood. Father's torch came bouncing in the dark.

She flung herself on him, arms around his neck, mouth at his ear. "It's in the house!" she whispered.

"The dwarf?"

She put her fingers on his mouth. The torch beam vanished.

Thud.

Father's arm tightened around Marion. She felt his muscles move nervously. Her anorak slid from his shoulders. He caught it and put it round her. She found the sleeves and slid her fists down inside.

Thud.

"We must get out!" shrieked Marion in the tiniest whisper.

"I've never seen a forty-stone dwarf," murmured Father. "I think a peek –"

"No –!"

Thud.

"Hush. You stay here –"

"No! No! No! You don't understand! The fear will kill you! Mr Merchantman died of fear!"

"His heart –"

"Daddy, I only survived because of what I am! We must leave! It pours out evil! It kills with wickedness! Why do you think there are no fish around the promontory! I saw ducks almost fall into the loch because of it!" She felt

111

Father shrink a little, as she had done.

Thud.

Marion faced the passage. A shadow lay in the light on the passage floor, but it was a shadow that made little sense to human eyes.

"We must go!" hissed Marion. "Out the front door!"

Father moved reluctantly. His fingers crept over Marion's hand and patted coldly.

"Wait a moment."

Thud.

The insides of the grandfather clock jingled.

"What are you doing!"

"Finding some change. Have you any coppers?"

"Money!" screamed Marion thinly.

"You must have some spare from shopping."

"Yes! Yes, here! What. . . ?"

Father took the coins in his cupped hand. He left Marion, blocking her view of the light from the kitchen, and the shadow that lay in the kitchen doorway. Suddenly he vanished.

"Daddy!"

Thud.

He rose like a ghost before her.

"It is a bit scary!" he gasped, and they fled, wellingtons fluffing, towards the front door.

The torch beam landed on the lock. Father's hand clicked the snib. He tugged. His fist grasped the door handle. Turned and tugged.

"Daddy!"

He turned the handle the other way.

"It won't open!"

The beam splashed to the top of the door. A closed bolt. Father's bare wrist, and fingers of jutting bone. Bang! went the bolt. Bang! went a second bolt at the bottom of the door. Turn the handle!

The floor shook.

Father groaned. He hauled fiercely.

The door wouldn't open.

16

Mother demands her change,
and Derek is shut out

"The mortise is locked! Without the key..."

Father's hands fell on Marion's shoulders pushing her towards the conservatory.

"Dong," said the clock staring down, and they scuttled away avoiding the dark mouth of the fireplace, pattering in rubber feet, cringing at the horrid *thud!* that shook the air, into the scent of earth and warm vegetation – the conservatory's skeleton a black cage with the winter sky beyond.

"There must be a door," gasped Father, peering desperately.

"There are so many plants!"

The beam flickered on greenery. They found a gap among the plants and a door with a fire escape bar holding it shut.

Father hit the bar with his palms. Marion

gasped at the noise, but the door moved – and jammed.

The torch beam swept the bar and stopped on a tangle of chain. "Padlocked!" cried Father. "Take the torch. Point it at the desk."

Thud! from across the great hall.

A scream pressed to escape from Marion's throat, but she pointed the torch gripping it in both fists, and Father ran carrying a captain's chair. "Stand aside!" He raised the chair, crashing it through the glass and timber wall of the conservatory.

Freezing air fell on them. Snowflakes rushed in speckling their faces.

A tremendous sound boomed through the house. The floor trembled. A pot plant toppled.

"Daddy!"

"Coins!" yelled Father. "Slippery little devils on a wooden floor! Out you go, my girl!"

"Coins!" gasped Marion. Snow welcomed her feet. Clever old Father! They ran. Towards the flat shine of the loch.

On the road, they trotted.

"Ha!" from Father, loud, but muffled by snow. "Wow! Fear, indeed!" he yelled. "It had me by the scruff of the neck, I can tell you! But we beat it! Didn't we beat it! oh, daughter of my wife!" Father dived for a snowball and hurled it into a garden. "The heavier they are,

115

the harder they fall! And that thing was heavy! Footprints in the snow! Y'saw me prodding into the footprints that went towards the castle? They sank through a good twenty centimetres of this beautiful, beautiful crystallized water – the pressure of each step melted the snow right down to the tarmac!"

He grabbed Marion, suddenly, holding her close to his jumper. "What the devil is it?" he whispered.

Marion unburied her face from Father's woolly grasp. She looked back along the road. Snowflakes dropped determinedly. Street lights glowed yellow. She shivered, and Father released her. They walked towards their gateposts.

"What's it about?" asked Father. Ardenlee's outside light whitened the drive. "Killing us seems a bit far-fetched."

Marion looked up at Father, and he smiled, snowflakes melting on his forehead, just the slightest bruise where Callum's torch had struck. His cheeks were thin with cold, his nose red.

"The boy can travel with his mind," said Marion. "And they hide themselves, Callum and the man, inside an area of power. It affects the fish –"

"Sandy mentioned the dead fish," said Father. "But if these two are hiding –" He guided Marion down the side of the house.

"– then they're up to something. Stands to reason. And Reason is our business. And that thing!" He opened the back door. "Well," he said firmly. "What a pleasant walk. Into the kitchen! Hello, Lizzie. Hello, my boy! Heat! Blessed calories! It's cold enough out there –"

"You've been gone twenty-nine and a quarter minutes," announced Derek.

"Really!" said Father.

"Are you reassured?" asked Mother, reaching for the coffee jar.

"Reassured?" asked Marion.

"Your father took you out to reassure you. And where's my change? Derek put down that biscuit."

"Oh. Father was very reassuring –"

"Change."

"I gave it to Father."

"I thought you were intelligent," said Mother.

"He! He!" said Father. "An intelligence quotient of a hundred and fifty-two is not to be sniffed at, Lizzie. That's six points up in four months. Plenty of mothers —"

"It's her other abilities that trouble me, John," said Mother quietly. "My IQ is not as high as Marion's or yours, but I know when something's going on. I would like to have enough of your respect, to be informed."

Marion looked from Mother to Father. Father smiled and dried his hair on the kitchen towel. His cheeks were warming, and his nose less red. Under the towel his eyes indicated Derek. "Anything worthwhile on the telly? Derek, pop through old son, and see if the fire needs a log. Your mother said no biscuits. Hop it, brat." Father grinned and hung up the towel.

"You're perfectly correct, Lizzie. Something is going on, but we don't know what. Don't you think you have enough to worry about? Unpacking—"

"I want to know!" Mother put mugs on the table, and the coffee smell made Marion shiver, then gulp, burning her tongue.

"We all have other qualities, Lizzie."

"What qualities?"

"Intellectual excellence ain't everything. You know that."

"I'm not stupid, John."

"We were just saying, Love is more important than Truth."

Mother's mouth opened, then shut, lips tight as Father talked on. "Love is also more important than an astronomical IQ. Some of the brightest men on the university scene are helpless outside a lecture theatre—"

"I want to know what's going on."

"I'm preparing the way," said Father quietly. "You know. Getting round to it. Gently. I don't want you frightened. You're the heart of this family—"

Derek returned. "There's only sport—"

"Go back through," said Father, and Derek retreated wordlessly under Father's gaze.

"You are the heart of this family." Father reached for Mother's hand. "There is something happening. But you must be strong—"

"What is it! John!"

"Lizzie, if you panic, I will not tell you."

Marion watched Mother's struggle to stay silent. Her mouth tightened into its rosebud shape. Father put his fingers on the rosebud, and Mother relaxed.

"Now," said Father. "What we know, is as follows. Marion will correct me as I go wrong. In the castle is a German and a boy named Callum. Which is a Scottish name. They have something to do with Sandy's mother. Around the castle is an area that wildlife shun — if we are to believe Sandy—"

"I saw ducks flying into a barrier," said Marion.

"And," said Father, "the boy has the same gift as Marion—"

"No!"

"It's true, Mother. He touched my mind when I was out with Derek. And there's something you don't know." Marion looked at her father. Mother's mouth opened and closed. The door creaked. Marion got up and pushed Derek gently all the way through to the study. "Please do what you're told," she said and returned, shutting doors. Then she recalled every moment of the invasion of the imps, and waited anxiously, as Father reasoned with Mother's fear.

"You wanted to know," Marion told her mother.

"But this!"

"Now, Lizzie. Keep calm. Hear the rest. Help us. We need you. If you are afraid. . ."

Mother breathed firmly. "I'm not afraid."

"That's my girl," murmured Father, and he stated quietly their adventure with the gargoyle.

Then he poured Mother a brandy.

"What I don't understand," he said, letting the words swell in the warm air of the kitchen, "is what the gargoyle is? A machine? I mean, Lizzie, it – is – so – bally – heavy!"

Snowflakes dropped past the black window. High in a corner, the bell waited, voiceless, a metal question mark, its wire clogged with paint.

"Do you remember Pardo?" breathed Marion.

"Pardo," said Father. "I saw him three days ago. Seems like a year. I told you about him, Lizzie. I remember the first day he strolled into the University. What a show-off! And what excitement for us! He just stood, hands in his pockets, his brown face fierce as the devil with concentration, making two ping-pong balls roll together over Farquharson's desk – then the panic to get the video set up. That man could lift pens, paper, rubbers, turn the pages of books. He's developed since then..." Father's voice died.

He turned slowly to Marion, gazing darkly. "Surely not?" he whispered.

Marion nodded.

"Telekinesis," breathed Father. "Of course. What point would there be in building a machine that moved so slowly and uselessly..."

"Telekinesis?" asked Mother. "I know what it is, but..."

"Pardo is telekinetic. He moves things with his mind. But not that statue...?"

"*They* can," said Marion. "But they don't just make the gargoyle move. The stone its legs are made of, changes position so the thing can walk. Molecular telekinesis. Callum and the German are a million times more powerful than Pardo."

17

---

*Mother tries to understand,
and Father hands her a letter*

"I don't think I understand." Mother blinked as if she might cry. "How can things move because someone wants...?"

"Lizzie, my dear." Father held Mother's plump fingers. "I know how impossible it sounds. And when you see it happen..." Father sighed. "Oh, Lizzie, it blows your mind! It's so ridiculous and there it is happening before your eyes! Huh! And people react in different ways. It's so important. A frontier of mind-power. And three-quarters of those who see it, deny it's happening. We were tricking them. Would you believe that? Tricking our students, our colleagues. The more open-minded accepted it, once it was proved. One girl fainted clean away. It's difficult, Lizzie, to take in. I know. And now we seem to be up against a highly-developed—"

"What do they want?" whispered Mother.

"They're interested in Marion."

"Interested?"

"Whatever they're up to, we think they are afraid Marion can interfere."

"And what will they do, John? Send her an invitation to a party?"

Father looked startled. "I'd forgotten that," he said.

So they talked, Father holding Mother's hand, assuring her that imps were an illusion. Insisting that telekinesis was a scientific fact. That the dead area around the castle was simply because fish and birds were sensitive to changes in the atmosphere; Marion noticed he didn't say what changes; that he didn't mention dead fish; and he avoided the devastating fear that surged from the gargoyle. . .

"Won't it come here?" asked Mother, both hands clutching Father's fingers. "It caused that old man to die."

"His heart—"

"Why did these terrible people send the gargoyle through his garden?"

"Oh." Father dug in his trouser pocket. He paused, his hand still in the pocket, rustling paper.

"You can't scare me more, John," said Mother, blinking anxiously.

Father withdrew his hand and flattened Jack Merchantman's letter on the table.

"You forgot to mention this," said Mother sharply, and turned the letter, pressing its creases with her soft fingers. She looked at Father and gulped. She rose, and returned to the table, nosing in her handbag. She shook spectacles free of a book of stamps that hung astride one leg.

Mother stared at Marion through the spectacles for such a time that Marion was embarrassed.

"I can't help what I am," she told her parents. "Don't you know how bad it's been for me? Can't you imagine? Nobody believing. Thinking I told lies. You thought I told lies, Mother. Until not so long ago when Father proved the truth in the laboratory. It's only the discipline Father has taught me, that stops me screaming. Only by control can I live a reasonably normal life. I am afraid. What will people ask me to do when they know I can go anywhere, unseen? Will everyone fear me? *They* know —"

Marion tilted her head towards the castle. "They *know*, and they're scared. There will be no end of people fearing me. So I must develop my power, control it! and use it for good! and be seen to use it for good! so that no one need *ever hide from me!*"

Marion felt her eyelids crinkle, and tears fell

over her lashes. Mother's warmth, smelling faintly of carrots, enclosed her, and Marion relaxed, weeping. Then she was hungry, and fingered a biscuit from the near-empty packet.

"I get so terrified," whispered Mother. "I forget you have it inside you. John," she said, in a voice that made Marion look intently at Mother's chubby face; eyes calm behind the spectacles; grown-up suddenly. "I won't be afraid. Not without good reason."

She sat very straight, and looked down at the letter. "It's addressed to the local paper.

SIR,

SINCE MY LETTERS DURING THE SUMMER MONTHS, PUBLISHED BY YOU, CONDEMNING THE LITTER LOUTS, HAD NO EFFECT, AND THE RAIN DID THE JOB OF KEEPING THOSE PEOPLE AWAY (SO MUCH FOR THE POWER OF THE PRESS!) I DON'T SUPPOSE THIS LETTER WILL CHANGE THE BE-HAVIOUR OF THE NEW RESIDENTS OF THE LOCH CASTLE. NOW, LADY FERGUSON, WHO I AM SURE IS A PERFECTLY NICE WOMAN, LIVES ON THE GROUND FLOOR AND I AM SAYING NOTHING AGAINST HER IN HER ANCESTRAL HOME, BUT THOSE IN THE UPPER FLOORS USE CHEMICALS AND PLAY MUSIC THAT WOULD BE AT HOME IN HELL! (I DON'T MEAN TO OFFEND ANYONE WITH MY LANGUAGE.) SINCE I LIKE TO SLEEP WITH MY BEDROOM WINDOW OPEN, WHICH IS MY RIGHT, AND I AM SURE NO ONE WILL DENY THIS, AND THESE PEOPLE INDULGE IN THEIR ANTISOCIAL

BEHAVIOUR AT NIGHT (AND DURING THE DAY!) I CANNOT SLEEP. IT IS AFFECTING MY HEALTH. NOTES PUSHED THROUGH THE DOOR HAVE BEEN IGNORED. NOW I AM AS PATIENT AS THE NEXT MAN, BUT I HAVE NOT SEEN A BIRD IN MY GARDEN FOR TWO (2) MONTHS AND I HAVE SEEN A YOUNG PERSON ON HER HORSE RIDING ON THE ROAD AT THE FRONT OF MY HOUSE AND VERY NEARLY BEING THROWN BECAUSE OF THE ANIMAL'S TERROR. SHE HASN'T YET SUCCEEDED IN PERSUAD-ING THE ANIMAL TO PASS THE CASTLE. I HAVE INFORMED THE INHABITANTS WITH A NOTE THROUGH THE DOOR THAT I AM WRITING THIS LETTER TO YOURSELF IN THE HOPE THAT SOMETHING MAY BE DONE. I DO NOT WISH TO BE A BAD NEIGHBOUR, BUT I AM AN OLD MAN AND LIKE MY COMFORTS. Nil desperandum. YOURS SINCERELY, JACK MERCHANTMAN.

P.S. THEY LAUGH AT ME ALL THE TIME, WHICH IS WORST."

Mother removed her spectacles.

Marion heard music penetrating from the study.

Father tipped his coffee cup, swirling the dregs. He sighed. "So the old boy told them. Put a note through the letterbox to let them know he was about to blab to the world. If the paper printed it."

"They sent the gargoyle?" said Marion.

"The postman saw its footprints," commented Father.

126

Mother continued to sit very straight. "Then they murdered him," she said.

"Unless," said Father quickly, "we are all quite dotty, and not observing accurately. Misinterpreting evidence. Loopy. Over-tired. Hungry."

"Oh, yes!" cried Marion. "Starved! Do I smell soup?"

"Just the tin of tomato," confirmed Mother.

"And Smash. . ."

"And Smash to save me peeling potatoes. Carrots, and a steak pie I bought in Keswick. . ."

Derek let music into the kitchen.

"Food won't be long," said Mother bravely.

18

*Marion takes up Father's suggestion
and finds Emptiness*

THURSDAY NIGHT

The sound of a log pushed into embers disturbed Marion. She woke to the firelit darkness of her bedroom.

Derek sprawled, one arm across Marion's chest. She eased him away, and raised her head to see over him. Father, still wearing his jumper, brushed wood dust and bark fragments into a corner of the hearth.

"Daddy."

"Thought you were asleep," whispered Father. "It's very late. Your mother's out for the count." He stopped brushing. "It's tough on our Lizzie, Marion. She's not as strong as you."

"I know."

"We ought to do something, my girl."

"You've got an idea?"

"You won't like it."

Father laid the brush on the hearth's green tiles. He rubbed his hands together. "You won't like it in the least."

"I might," breathed Marion.

"Go to the castle," said Father suddenly. "Find out what's going on. Without knowledge we can't act. They've made every move so far and all we do is run. We must know —"

"I can't!" Marion huddled under the bedclothes. She heard Father come round the bed, and crouch beside her.

"I'll be right here."

She turned towards him, and he stroked her hair.

She lay still, her eyes open to the flickering darkness, Father's jumper a woolly protection from her fears; the rhythm of his fingers on her hair.

"I can't."

The stroking became a pat. "All right," said Father.

"Is it?" She snatched at his hand. "Is it all right?"

"Sure."

"What will you do?"

"Well. . ." Father's smile caught the firelight. "Think again, I suppose."

The log flared, throwing a red glow across Father's brow. "One thing," he said. "In the morning, I'll pop along to Jack Merchant-man's house. Make sure it's secure. The plants, you know. Repair the conservatory, if I can. I expect a lot of plants will die in this cold." Father grinned. "And retrieve Mother's change from the hall floor." Marion slapped his arm.

Then Father said goodnight, and Marion faced the fire, her cheek on her palm, Derek breathing.

She loved the firelight with the sudden shifts of logs, and smoke squirting from the wood's interior. Shadows raged on the hearth.

Marion lay back.

Darkness dodged firelight on the ceiling.

What would Father do? He was right. Knowledge was needed to solve any problem. But was it right to intrude? Marion let her eyes close.

The loch lay deep among the mountains. The air stood thick with falling snow. On the flat water, the promontory rested. Seaweed and mussel-clusters skirted the rock. Nothing moved.

The rock's face cut the water's surface and descended to an underwater landscape of boulders, like men's heads with hair flowing green. Silt drifted in currents. Crab shells tumbled emptily. Dead fish hung in the depths, some descending, some rising as the gases of decay inflated their skins. A dog's skeleton rocked its skull. Nothing lived.

The mussels on the promontory clacked faintly in a swirl of black water. The castle towered in white rags, burying its head in the dropping air. Fear touched Marion's thoughts, so that her mind staggered.

She recalled vaguely, her first probing of the castle as she stood on the beach with Derek; and the fear of death.

But now she reflected the fear back on itself, and entered the castle.

She fled from room to room through dust and emptiness, the silent walls, longing, it seemed, for laughter.

Then a room blazed at her with electric heat, and she recoiled from a bed mountainous with the sleeping German.

In another room the boy slept with dreams on his lips. Marion descended close to his face and he sat up suddenly, then relaxed back, still asleep.

She searched until her mind wept with the dreariness of evil.

She searched until she despaired of finding the heart of the castle. Then a blessing flowed from her, to the boy, and she felt a barrier dissolve so that she entered a room with grand windows filled with snow and darkness. And on the bare floor a painted circle, with symbols familiar to her from Father's books, though she did not know their meaning. And in the circle, a long stool, richly carved in black

131

wood; and around the stool, a spread of clean sand; then something dented the sand as a fish's belly might dent sand beneath the waters of the loch. And something fluttered as a bird flutters in a cage. But there *was* no bird. And no fish.

Then fear wrapped its arms around Marion, and she fled beyond the castle enjoying the clean world; until out of the snow-filled night, something rushed on her.

19

*Mother sings,
and Father is startled*

Marion opened her eyes to firelight gleeful on the ceiling.

She reached and felt Derek, warm and breathing.

She slept until cold woke her and the room was grey with dawn. Father's voice sang in the bathroom.

Marion rolled out of bed and rushed to the fire, but the grate was soft with ash. A spider paced across the hearth and she warned it not to linger for the fire would be lit in the afternoon.

Then underwear and cord trousers sprang onto Marion's body from her fast hands. She dived ceilingwards into her baggy jumper. Stomped into warm boots. Brushed her hair so that it stirred with electricity. She danced rather desperately until Father left the bathroom. No way would she sit in the icy toilet below the stairs. Wow! for summer, thought Marion, but, truly, she was invigorated. She threatened Derek with a wet face cloth, but he groaned and curled beneath the covers. Anyway, there were things to say, and Derek asleep, was Derek not-listening.

In the kitchen, breakfast smells rose around Mother, and the first *dunt!* of the axe sounded outside. Marion ran into the bright white morning, and smiled at Father, and he grinned. She smiled at the coach-house soft-roofed with snow, and the trees stolen from a Christmas card. A *whoosh!* took her glance to the hothouse and Father paused, looking round, loosening his leather jacket, as pillow-thick snow hung over the hothouse gutter, then whumped! onto the ground. Father's grin spread delight around the garden, and Marion ran, touching snow, examining snow on the iron pineapples atop the clothes poles.

On the house wall the blue phone cable dangled.

Dunt! said the axe, and the split wood released its scent. Marion darted, away from Father, down the side of the house, glimpsing smoke from Sandy's chimneys next door. She dashed beside shrubbery, towards the gateposts and welcome! wide went Marion's arms as she embraced the loch in its winter glory; the white mountains. Already the red and white ferries crossed each other on the distant estuary. And "Ooh? Ooh?" asked the eider-ducks, and gulls paced the beach and flapped a wing's length, while rooks busied among boulders.

Marion yelled with joy, and the gulls rose then settled lazily on the loch. The sun, a balloon, pale behind the house, strained to warm the landscape, but road, water and hills slept tight beneath their winter blanket, deaf to the quack! of a duck in flight, and unconscious of ripples murmuring on the beach.

A red van cruised, stopping, and George said, "Good morning!" fingering letters-in-a-bundle, but there was nothing. And nothing, he assured Marion, for the old man who had died. Marion smiled, relieved. No one other than the postman, surely, could discover the broken conservatory?

Then Father strolled beside her, slim and handsome in his leather jacket; a gleam of sweat on his brow, a smile for his daughter. "Breakfast's ready," he said. So they walked round the house, past splinters of logs in the snow, and logs in a heap, into the kitchen, where coffee and bacon scented the air, and Mother tra-la-d to Radio 2, and shuffled plates of food to the table.

"Well now," said Mother. "See how brave I

am? Singing?" She tilted her head, thoughts in a frown, then smiled. "What's to be done?"

"I've done something," said Marion, and Father paused in buttering his toast. "What you said, Daddy. I didn't intend to. I closed my eyes and went into the loch. There's nothing alive near the castle. And in the castle. Such emptiness. Such ... *lack*. As if people were working very hard, and the harder they worked, the more life was taken from them. They have a circle painted on the floor, with sand spread in it, and full of energy. I sensed fish, and perhaps a bird. But like ghosts of fish and birds. I was afraid. This is where the feeling of death is. I felt it that first time – when I was with Derek on the beach. Yesterday?"

"The day before," said Father quietly.

"Something rushed at me."

"What!" Father dropped his knife. "What d'you mean?"

"Something rushed at me. It came from this direction."

"A bird?" asked Mother, wiping butter off the table where it had jumped from Father's knife.

"It was really strange," said Marion, shaking her head at Mother's question.

"Hold on," said Father finishing spreading. "You haven't experienced this before?"

"Eat your bacon," said Mother gently.

"I'm not sure. So many subtle things

happen. Like bits of dreams. Perhaps they are bits of dreams. But this was real."

"It could be important," said Father. "Remember," he urged.

"Couldn't she. . . ?" Mother's fork gestured at Marion's plate, but Father's head shook and he stared at Marion.

"Remember."

She closed her eyes, resting her cutlery. She felt the knife and fork pulled from her fingers. She saw snow falling and glimpsed trees in nearby gardens. She sensed again her fear as turmoil rushed on her.

"What does it look like?"

"It has no appearance."

"Does it disturb the snowflakes?"

Snowflakes dropped steadily.

"No."

"Is it coming towards you, or the castle?"

"Both." Marion opened her eyes. She ate. Father cut his egg, letting the yolk run out.

"No sign of Lazy Bones," said Mother, glancing at the ceiling.

Father's mouth smiled, but silence was the background to the scrape of knives.

Feet thudded outside in the snow. Someone passed the window. Father turned as the outer door opened. The kitchen door burst in and Sandy gaped stupidly, panting, a holly leaf on her jumper, a scratch across her cheek.

She stepped towards Father and held out her hands.

"Oh, John!" she whispered.

Father put down his knife and fork.

He took her hands.

Sandy's face crumpled, her mouth hauled into a dreadful gape.

"*Help me!*" she wailed.

20

Father discloses his theory,
and Marion talks about Sandy's father

LATER ON FRIDAY MORNING

"I feel like a criminal," groaned Father, and Marion patted the bag he carried – a leather bag, clinking with tools.

Father glanced back towards Ardenlee, then teetered elegantly on tiptoe peering ahead towards the castle. "The Old Bill abaht?" he demanded in a cockney accent. "You'll like 'Olloway, my gel. Your muvva enjoyed it, and your granmuvva –"

"Stop it!" giggled Marion. "The Old Bill won't send us to Holloway for repairing Mr Merchantman's conservatory. Watch you don't slip. You shouldn't fool about when Sandy's mother. . ."

"Poor Sandy! What a shock. But that doctor appeared smartly. He thought the old lady was dead, until he'd had a good listen. Let's hope the snow plough clears the hill so the ambulance—"

"Will she die?"

"I don't know, Marion. Her electric blanket kept her alive. She was comatose. Been like that most of the night the doctor thought. . ."

Father strode quickly. "Perhaps," he said loudly, "she went into the coma at the time something rushed at you outside the castle."

"What do you mean?"

"A circle represents endlessness," lectured Father. "Round and round it goes. There's no exit. The fact that there isn't a brick wall to keep in the contents, doesn't matter. The circle is a symbol powerful enough to restrain, just as a word from a headmaster is powerful enough to restrain. Do you know what I think?"

He stopped, and looked down at Marion.

"I think that the fish and birds you sensed, were really there. At least, their energy was. I think that what you felt rushing at you last night was energy drawn from Sandy's mother. I think that the people in the castle want to live for ever."

They walked.

Marion protesting.

Then she recalled that Sandy's mother had said her husband would never die, and she was silent.

They entered Jack Merchantman's drive.

Timbers jutted where Father had broken the conservatory. They looked in at the captain's chair dropped by Father. Plants hung miserably in the cold air.

"Let's go to the back door," murmured Father.

They wandered between outbuildings, detecting dimples in the snow left by their own feet last night. And other feet.

The back door gaped. Snow whitened the kitchen linoleum. Marion followed Father inside, and she felt *watched*. As if pots and dishes had turned to stare.

Sausages lying in their own juice, made a limp hand by the cooker.

Father dug in his leather bag, found Jack Merchantman's torch and led Marion into the gloom of the passageway.

"See this floor?" said Father. "Quarter-cut oak. Cut a log one way – it's not as strong as it might be. Cut it another... You could drive a tank over this floor. Ah! Our coins!" The light showed Mother's change.

"Look," said Father, and Marion fingered dents in the floorboards. "These are new," said Father, and smiled rather grimly. "Look around the floor. Hardly a mark. Generations of feet and furniture, and nothing has damaged it. Until last night. What that thing must weigh! No wonder the house shook when it slipped on our coins. What's this?" He picked up something dark, then passed it to Marion. It was a green pad the size of one of the coins.

"Moss," said Marion.

"Fresh, too," said Father. He sighed, shaking the money in his palm. "I wish I understood," he whispered. "Come on. The conservatory awaits!"

They hurried through the hall, huddling nervously as the clock whirred as if about to speak, but its hands said five-past eleven, and the whirr subsided, leaving shadows listening and doors open with people behind them. But there was really no one, and Marion walked at Father's heels into the conservatory.

The captain's chair was returned to its place at the desk. Snow was scraped from the floor and dropped outside. Fingertips gathered glass shards and stacked them beside a dustbin.

The conservatory grew whole again as Father worked. "Not as good as new," he admitted. "However, there's still heat on somewhere, so maybe the plants will recover. And the grandfather clock has chimed several times so I ought to be hungry. Marion? What's wrong? Marion!"

21

*Father finds something to laugh about,
and a black car visits Sandy*

Sniggering in an empty room.

Marion stared, horrified, into the sitting room that spread gloomily beyond the french windows.

"Don't you hear it?" she whispered.

Father turned his gaze from her.

Among the daylight shadows, sniggering.

Father's fingers tightened into the flesh of Marion's arm. The hair on Marion's neck prickled, for nothing human, except herself and Father, moved in Mr Merchantman's house.

"Did someone come in?" breathed Father. "Did you hear someone come in? Are they behind the furniture? Marion—"

Marion found Father's hand, and eased his grip from her arm. "There's no one."

"Time to smash our way out through the

conservatory again!" squeaked Father in a whisper, then he breathed deeply, and Marion looked at him, and his eyes, though bright, searched fearlessly. He even grinned a little on his daughter, and his daughter touched his cheek with cold fingertips; and though fear crawled under her skin, Marion stepped with Father towards the french windows to go into the sitting room, while the sniggering sped around the conservatory walls, gentle as spiders, swift as a breeze.

Father held Marion back as the sound approached and passed.

"What do we do?" she gasped.

"Is this for our benefit?" panted Father, "or is it left over from Jack Merchantman's time?"

"What do you mean?"

"I mean, daughter, that the old chap mentioned someone laughing at him – in his letter to the editor. Is this a continuation – or the first manifestation?"

The sniggering hurried around the walls again. "Feel the fear?" said Father. "Same as last night when the gargoyle walked. Fear is their weapon –"

"Sandy's mother," whispered Marion. "She heard laughter in her room. Thought it was the cat."

"Is – that – so?" said Father, and he took Marion's wrist firmly, and with the torch feeble in the soft daylight, he stepped through the french windows into the sitting room.

A great breath of laughter, ghastly and jeering swept around them, but Father stood, hand clamped on Marion's bones, watching, waiting till the noise died. Then he took her into the centre of the room. Marion found strength in his courage.

He strode among the furniture, dragging her with him, pointing the torch into pools of gloom. "Hither and thither," thought Marion. And her fear slipped away, though the sounds continued.

Father smiled with his dark eyes, and released her wrist. He sat calmly in an armchair and indicated another chair. Marion walked three paces alone and sat, trying to smile. She grinned – probably like a lunatic, she thought. And the laughter soared dreadfully, knotting her muscles, but Father beamed and Marion grinned fiercely, her flesh rippling with loathing at the mockery and gurglings.

"Shouldn't we leave?" she whispered.

"Leave?" said Father loudly. "Not when we're enjoying ourselves. Ha! Ha! Ha! Does y'good to laugh! Ha! Ha! Ha! Ha!" His finger encouraged Marion and she laughed, and the sound hesitated.

Then a silence listened around the walls.

Father's lips stretched across his teeth. "So much for fear," he murmured.

"So much for fear!" gasped Marion, but she

sat rigid, while Father returned to the conservatory.

She heard the click of tools and he came carrying the leather bag, Jack Merchantman's torch in his hand, and Marion followed close to his grey jacket, glad he was her father; glad he had overcome fear.

Thankful to leave the haunted house.

A breeze sparkled on the loch.

"Another round to us, I think," said Father.

Clink said the leather bag.

Marion smiled.

They strode cheerfully. A snowball landed at Marion's feet, and a snigger made her gasp.

Then she knew it was really a giggle, and something like an elbow inside an anorak moved behind the stone gatepost of Ardenlee.

"Rein back the hosses!" cried Father. "We're under attack! Don't shoot until ya see the red of their noses!"

He dropped his bag and Marion joined Father in lobbing snowballs over the gatepost. Shrieks of delight arose from the shrubbery, and a little fist flickered, darting a snowball onto the pavement no more than a step from the giggling Indian.

Marion laughed, and ducks rattled across the loch. Derek leapt into view, threw two snowballs violently, but they broke in flight, and he growled among his giggles, running at

Marion, pummelling her with his fists until Father asked him to count how many chimneys were smoking.

And the landscape was beautiful, thought Marion, with the smoke standing above so many grand houses all along the shore; the smoke from some thick and white because fires were newly lit, but rippling blue from fires kindled early. Even across the loch where houses sat small as a fingernail, threads of smoke were drawn on the hillside.

Derek counted, and Father pointed out some he'd missed, so the counting began again. A car bobbed distantly on the snowy road from the village and vanished behind a bend. It reappeared closer, a black car, but not as large, decided Marion, as a Mercedes.

The car slowed carefully, blink-blinking into Sandy's drive.

"The doctor," said Father. "I hope it's not bad news."

22

*Marion dances,
and says "Boo!" to a ghost*

"Look, you two—" Father pointed at the leather bag on the pavement. "—would you put that in the coach-house? I'll see if Sandy needs anything. Off you go. A handle each." Father patted Derek's bottom, and Marion helped Derek carry the bag.

"Why has Father gone next door?"

"You heard. To see if Sandy needs anything. Her mother's not well."

"Is she dying?"

Marion sighed and wondered why little brothers were so gruesome. "Maybe," she said quietly.

She stopped walking, making Derek stop.

They stood in the driveway, Derek frowning at Marion, for he knew when something trod on her soul.

Marion examined the garden.

The sunken lawn filled with snow, was damaged by a trail of Derek's footholes.

The three steps up from the grass to the gravel patio were soft as pillows. Shrubs and trees waited for spring, hanging in white silence.

She lowered the bag, and left Derek. She stood between the stone posts and gazed at the beach.

On the beach, towards the shops, a party of terns – like little seagulls – huddled nervously. Coots came paddling, as if something unseen chased them from the direction of the promontory; as if the dead area around the castle had spread suddenly, to include Ardenlee. She crossed the road, and stared along the green tide-mark on the beach.

Towards the shops roamed the seabirds. Towards the castle. . .

Marion turned, looking for Derek. He stood in the drive beside Father's bag, his face round and pink above his anorak.

"Derek!" Wings heaved at the crack of her voice. "Come here!"

He came.

"What do you see?" she demanded, nodding along the beach towards the castle.

"Nothing." Derek jumped down onto rocks and threw a stone at the water. The stone rattled among boulders.

"Is there anything alive?" whispered Marion.

"No." Another stone bounced, splashing into the loch. "Can't you see?"

"I can see," sighed Marion.

The dead area around the castle had increased – just now – to include Ardenlee. She thought of Sandy's mother, and shivered. Perhaps her death – if she *was* dead – had increased the power at the castle.

Derek found a tin, and took it to the water's edge. He dropped a tiny pebble inside as Father had shown him, then set the ship nodding in its ocean, properly ballasted. He fired stone rockets, and Marion launched a stone missile, wobbling the target. Far away, a fishing boat tore a white line in the loch. Gulls were sprinkled above it, like salt on the mountains.

Father's voice.

Marion turned. Father beckoned from Sandy's gate and she hurried, leaving Derek on the beach.

"Have you warned your mother?"

"We haven't been in yet –"

"Tell her to come through!"

"The birds –"

"Now! Please. The old lady has just died."

"Oh."

Marion stepped back from Father. She was sorry about Sandy's mother, but more sorry about Father's anger. Sandy's mother, after all, was only a peculiar person who sat in the dark, and told lies to visitors.

She ran in her wellingtons, lifting the tool bag, silly tears wetting her eyes. She dumped the bag in the utility room, dried her face, blew her nose, then found Mother in the study. The fire stood tall with flames, the television talked to itself, and Mother slept with a cup loose in her hand, and sugar on her fingers.

Mother woke. "Oh!" she said. "Oh. Is this fire safe? You stay here Marion. I must find a pair of shoes. Did you see Derek? Poor Sandy. What a blow. You stay here –"

"Yes, Mother. I'll look after the house."

Mother went in search of shoes.

Marion switched off the television and watched logs burning, listening to their gassy music, breathing their smell of woodland. She heard the back door close as Mother left. In the kitchen, she found home-made doughnuts.

She returned to the fire, eating, drinking milk, wishing the old lady had died after lunch time.

A spark arched down to the hearth.

Marion licked the sugar from her thumb, removed her wellingtons, practised a pas de deux through to the dining room, and discovered a fireguard protecting the carpet from the hot murmuring prisoner under the black mantelpiece.

The fireguard was dented and its brass mesh stained green with age. Marion thought Father must have found it in the coach-house. Or in the loft while he was looking for the drip above the melted basin. She twirled beautifully and staggered.

Derek laughed somewhere.

He was always sneaking.

She twirled again, but the carpet chugged her feet and she almost fell.

Derek sniggered, and Marion invented a horrible face.

She presented the face to the door.

The snigger chittered around the room, but Derek was still on the other side of the door. The door lay open the width of her palm.

She jerked it wide and said, "Boo!"

Then she remembered that Derek was on the beach.

23

Marion is alone,
and something moves among the trees

Marion stood silent as the awful noise tittered around the room behind her.

"Derek?" she breathed hopefully.

She crossed the passage and entered the heat of the kitchen. Her heart throbbed, telling her to run, but she clung to a chair and decided to laugh as Father had laughed. But her throat crushed the laughter and tears ran to the corners of her mouth.

She fled into the utility room and hauled at the back door. The handle rattled in her grasp. Cold air blew over her stockinged feet. She blinked at the lock. The round end of the key filled the keyhole.

Mother had locked the door on the outside.

The draught under the door froze Marion's ankles. Tears dashed onto her woolly sleeves as she shook the handle, and the snickering flowed from the dining room, a vast laughter filling the kitchen.

She screamed. Then the laughter ceased, and Marion, startled, strangled her scream, but her breath moaned in her mouth.

Then she heard an echo of her breath. Or someone panting behind the central heating boiler. But between the boiler and the wall was space enough only for a man's arm. Certainly no one could hide.

Marion remembered laughing in Jack Merchantman's house, *deciding* – more or less – not to be afraid.

"I am not afraid."

The breathing behind the boiler stopped.

Marion stood still.

Had she won already? It seemed too easy.

She stepped into the kitchen and lifted the phone. Silence filled her ear. She remembered the snapped cable.

A cardboard box sat open-mouthed on the floor displaying bags of flour and a dented custard tin. How far away their kitchen in London seemed now. She replaced the phone. The brass bell hung like a question mark high on the wall.

Minutes passed, and because nothing sniggered, Marion relaxed, though tears changed the kettle into a cream and black-topped blob.

She made coffee, and sat with it at Father's table. She still wanted to run, but the house was a good house. The coffee ran hot into her stomach.

She wondered if all the phones in the village were out of order. Sandy's phone had crackled. And their own phone before the lorry came. Was the dead area affecting the lines?

She looked out of the kitchen window.

The snow's edges had softened in the sun. The hothouse roof shone dark where snow had slipped. The coach-house, Marion thought, was perfect, with its old-fashioned green doors and red brick chimneys. A robin would complete the scene.

But no birds moved.

Trees raised wooden wrists waiting for the flutter of wings.

But no birds moved.

Raspberry canes grew cages where feathered bodies could run.

But no birds moved.

Marion sent her mind onto the snow. The surface glittered like damp salt, rising with each bump of the earth, and humped on plants, or punctured by grass. Roots arched like frozen snakes.

Trees flowed past Marion, as her imagination took her through the Plantation.

The Plantation spread behind the houses.

A stream foamed through reeds. A railway sleeper was a bridge, snow-thick and slippery to a human foot; but the girl sped on.

155

Branches held deserted nests. Beneath a rotting wheelbarrow, a chrysalis dangled on a single thread, ugly, the living dead, nature's vampire awaiting the sun. And on she swam hearing nothing but snow slipping, and once, coal on a shovel in a coal shed, and the cough of a dog too civilized to sense the desert around the castle.

She fled higher among branches, seeing just one leaf on a sycamore and furry sleeves of moss on ancient oaks, spiders' webs magically delicate in the descending sun, delicately deadly to an insect's tread. But no insect moved.

And no birds stirred.

Marion looked down on Jack Merchantman's house. She saw the conservatory, with Father's mended framework. Trees crowded the castle rock, and the rock stood high holding the castle in arrogance above the countryside.

Among the trees, something moved.

It wasn't a bird.

24

*Lady Ferguson offers escape
and Father carries a pole*

Marion pushed fear aside and watched,
listening, to the crash of branches, to a thud!
thud! on the mouldering leaves, quicker, she
thought, quicker, she knew, than the clunk of
the gargoyle.

Then she realized that not only had the dead
area grown since Sandy's mother had died, but
the power of the gargoyle had increased. And
the thud! among the trees was the dreadful
weapon striding with new energy towards
Marion's home.

She saw movement and a tree shook, snow
dropping from its branches.

She waited (in her mind), by the sleeper that
bridged the stream and wished desperately for
telekinetic power like Pardo at the University –
power to knock the sleeper into the water.

The sleeper stretched white between the

banks of the stream. Surely a thing that slid on coins would slide on that?

Thud! Thud! Branches breaking.

The day darkened, leaving snow dull and cold.

Flakes descended through the trees.

Thud! Thud! Dared she wait to see it? with its stone legs pounding! Thud! Thud! its stone eyes, and stone wings like a great rucksack heaped white?

She fled, instantly beneath the wheelbarrow, where the chrysalis dangled on its thread. Yellow toadstools perkily sprouted from the barrow's rotten timber.

CRASH! Like a great rock falling into the stream.

Marion opened her eyes, staring at the garden beyond the kitchen window. The gargoyle, she knew, had slipped on the bridge.

A dog howled.

Marion ran to the study, sat on the rug and pulled on her wellingtons. She noticed the fire settling to a steady flicker. It was safe to leave. She went to the utility room for her anorak. She stared at the telephone, then thumped through to the hall and opened the front door.

A woman stood in the drive.

Marion said, "Oh!" not knowing whether to go inside, shutting the woman out, or rush past her. She let the door slam at her heels, then hurried towards the stranger, stopping out of reach.

"My mother's not in."

"I am Mary Ferguson," said the woman urgently. "Lady Ferguson! Do you understand! Are you the child? Speak! If you are not, I am wasting time! Are you the child?"

"Yes—"

The woman stepped closer. She was older than Father, prettier than Mother. Her tweed coat met the tops of her wellingtons. Green wellingtons, like Father's, but scuffed. A headscarf captured snowflakes on printed apples.

"You must leave now. I have stolen money from them." Her fist thrust at Marion. "Run to Tigh-na-Mara, the third house past the shops. Say that Mary Ferguson sent you. Dan will drive you to Glasgow. You must have relatives. . ."

Marion retreated.

"Take the money!" Lady Ferguson's eyes commanded and pleaded. "Take it, child. There is no time—"

"Excuse me!" gasped Marion, and dodged the fist that offered money. She ran along the drive.

"You must!"

Marion raced between the gateposts. She looked for Derek, and saw him crouched among seabirds far along the shore. She strode up Sandy's drive. The doctor's car was gone. The front door opened as Marion thudded up the steps. Father's solemn face looked out at her.

"She's taking it on the chin," said Father. "Poor Sandy. There's a sensitive woman under that —"

"It's coming!" gritted Marion.

Father stared.

"I think it's stuck in the stream. And Lady Ferguson's here. She offered me money. Told me to go to Glasgow."

"Glasgow? Lady Ferguson? Is she at our house?"

"They were sniggering —"

Footsteps hurried on the drive. Marion turned, recognizing the sound of wellingtons.

"I'll talk to her," said Father. "Your mother's in the kitchen."

"Daddy, there's no time!"

"If it's stuck in the stream we have a few minutes. Maybe Lady Ferguson knows something that will help. Get inside."

Marion paused in the hall.

She heard Mother and Sandy talking in the kitchen, and outside, Father's greeting cut short by Lady Ferguson.

Marion gazed at the books on the sideboard. She carefully translated German titles: *Mind Over Mind* by *von Gors*. *Psychometry in the Aryan Race* by *Nikolas Dansk*.

"He is Sandy's father!" shrieked Lady Ferguson.

Marion stared at the outside door.

Father and Lady Ferguson were one shape on the coloured glass panel.

Who could Lady Ferguson mean? Surely the German wasn't Sandy's father?

"He divorced Sandy's mother!" raged Lady Ferguson, "then against my wishes, he married my daughter! Callum is my daughter's child! My grandson!"

Marion turned, stunned, from the door.

The bulk of water in the oil painting, threatened her. Then she realized that Callum was the son the German needed to work his miracles.

She burst into the kitchen.

Cold air made Sandy shiver. Father and Lady Ferguson crowded in at Marion's back.

"What's wrong?" cried Mother. "John?"

"Lizzie," said Father catching Mother's hands. "No time for questions. No time for hesitating—"

"Oh!"

"—Derek's on the beach. Go and get him. Bring him here. Run Lizzie! Off you go! Sorry, Sandy!" cried Father. "Lady Ferguson will explain. As if you don't have enough on your plate. Good thing Marion told you about herself! Come on, my girl!"

Marion ran after him through the hall. "It will come here!" she shouted.

"You said they were sniggering at you

in the house?"

"Yes—"

"Probably just another scaring session! Then they saw you were alone and sent the gargoyle. It's heading for Ardenlee to finish you!" Father shut Sandy's outside door. "Mother and Derek'll be safe here."

Marion remembered wondering if she had beaten the sniggering too easily.

"Why are we going round the side of the house?"

"Remember the junk we moved from the laundry room?"

"Yes."

"Mind the holly. Through the hedge. There's something I want."

They emerged from the wedding trees onto their own drive.

"Listen," said Father.

Snow fell steadily.

Thud! faint in the Plantation.

"It's coming!" whispered Marion.

"Go! Head for the castle! Go!" Father sped towards the coach-house.

Marion hurried down the drive.

She found a fresh tyre track and ran along it.

Why was she going to the castle? It wouldn't do to arrive without Father. She stopped.

She stared back through the dropping flakes.

Father emerged from the white weather, striding, staggering under the weight of the

162

iron clothes pole which rested on the shoulder of his grey jacket.

"What are you doing with that!"

"Go on! Run!"

His face was white.

"It's too heavy!" shouted Marion.

"I'll tell you when I need help!" snarled Father, and Marion fled, weeping suddenly, Father gasping behind her.

Marion saw headlights creeping.

She turned. "There's a car coming!"

Father staggered off the road and tried to run on the pavement but the pole slipped, ripping the shoulder from his jacket. He fell.

Marion ran at the vehicle waving her arms.

It stopped with Marion facing the driver's door.

The window was thick with snow.

The door began to open.

"Marion?" George stared anxiously from the post office van.

"Help Daddy!" gasped Marion.

Father was struggling to lift the pole. "Can you take us to the castle?"

"Well. . ."

"D'you know that Sandy's mother is dead?" demanded Father.

George gaped.

"Dead?" he whispered.

"Sandy couldn't phone you. The phones are

all out. The doctor was coming anyway. . . Oh, I'm sorry, George!" urged Father. "You must help us!"

George stared at the green-painted clothes pole with its pineapple top and rusted base. He dashed his hand across his eyes. "Dead, you say? She died?"

Marion shook the postman's arm. "We can't explain now! We think the German killed her! The German is Sandy's father!"

George staggered as if Marion had struck him. Horror slackened his face. He towered over Marion.

"Killed my Bess!" he whispered. "Sandy's father? Oh, no. Oh, he was Bess's husband. I see that now — though he is sorely changed — but . . ."

The postman gazed down at Marion.

". . .*I* am Sandy's father."

25

Father puts the clothes pole to good use,
and George puts it to better use

The van slid to a halt in the lane beside the castle.

Father said, "I'm sorry, George. I had no idea that you and Sandy's mother were that close. We thought —"

"No one knew," said George. His gaze bored up at the castle. "Except him. And he wasn't sure. All he wanted was a boy. But Bess could have only one child, and that was Sandy. So there *was* no boy.

"Then he left. And now he has returned. And he has his revenge." George faced Father. "Why are you involved?"

"I don't know if you'll understand this," said Father, "but Marion is psychic –"

"I understand, Professor Kent. I understand perfectly. Let's get your clothes pole, shall we?"

And they carried the clothes pole over the low gate.

Marion shuddered. The last time she and Father had been here, the gargoyle had stood beside the balustrade.

"Lady Ferguson gave me her keys." Father unlocked the door at the top of the steps. He led quickly to a great kitchen. "There are servants' stairs somewhere. Leading to all floors. Here we are."

George and Father carried the pole between them, up the narrow staircase.

Marion paused, peering through a slit window at the snowy roofs of Jack Merchantman's house.

They stopped at a landing while Father examined a door.

"Keep going," said Father.

Another landing, with another door.

Father nodded upwards, gasping, and they ascended.

"This is it!" whispered Father. "See. Oil on the hinges. And a spyhole. Lady Ferguson liked to know what was going on."

The postman's large hand whitened around the clothes pole.

"You know what to do," panted Father. "Break the circle with the pole. Iron is a traditional defence against magic. It also happens to be an excellent conductor of energy. Same thing, I suppose. Let's get it over."

He slid a key into the lock. "Marion, you stay here. I only brought you so that the gargoyle would head back towards the castle and leave everyone else safe. You with me George? Glad of a bit of company. I think the heebie-jeebies are creeping up. Forward!" he whispered. And grinning dismally, Father opened the door and strolled in, the pole hanging between him and George.

The grand windows stood pale with daylight.

A fireplace roared red-hot.

The circle still contained sand, and in the middle of the sand, on the carved stool sat Callum and the German. Callum, a splinter of a boy, his head too heavy almost, for his neck, and the man, squatting gigantically.

Father hesitated. "They're concentrating so hard," he said quietly, "that they don't know we're here. They soon will! Ready?"

The clothes pole swung forward, then back.

"Go!"

It crashed short of the circle.

The German's fingers moved.

"Come on, George!" gasped Father.

They slid the pole into the sand.

Marion's skin tingled.

Father rubbed his face. "A release of energy!" he gasped.

Callum moaned. The giant's arms straightened. His head turned, and Marion stared, for though the eyes wandered, the strength in that terrible face startled her.

The German rose, truly gigantic.

He saw the pole. Then his gaze found Marion, and gathered her up.

"No y'don't!" whispered Father, but the monstrous figure lumbered at Marion, knocking Father aside, ignoring George.

A hand groped for her throat. Behind the giant, Marion saw George duck suddenly, and she heard the clothes pole scrape.

Fingers touched her neck.

George rose.

Callum shrieked.

Iron struck bone.

Silence; and the fire merrily jigging.

Silence; and the daylight cool on the heap that was the fallen giant.

Then Callum ran – shrilling dreadful words – to cradle the massive head.

Father shook Marion. "Do something!"

She stared at him.

"Help them!"

"Help them? *They want to kill me!*" she shrieked.

"Help them!" commanded Father.

She stared into Father's dark gaze.

Marion knew, suddenly, that she had much to learn about being The Kindest Person in the World.

So – though her heart was cold – she

reached out her thoughts and lowered them over Callum.

She warmed him with love.

Energy broke from the boy's mind, startling her. But she absorbed it. Then she spread her love to the man.

Joy poured out of her.

She forgave.

She released them.

The boy wept over his father.

Marion whispered, "He's alive."

Father strode away from her, into the circle, kicking up fountains of sand. He lifted the stool and hurled it against a wall. He marched to the window and faced the cold daylight.

George opened his mouth to speak.

Father turned suddenly and stared at Marion. He looked at George. "You saved her life," he whispered.

ONE SUNDAY, THE FOLLOWING SUMMER

Sunshine roasted the plum trees.

Beyond the bottom of the garden, at the edge of the Plantation, Marion knew that a statue stood. An awful statue, with wings that no longer held snow, but sheltered a blackbird's nest. Tendrils of ivy covered the statue's feet, and fragments of winter reeds, which grew only in the stream, were pressed into cracks in the stony body.

Father's deckchair creaked, and Marion looked at him. His eyes flickered shut against the sun. "We missed a great opportunity, my girl."

Marion heard Sandy calling through the shrubbery to Derek.

"I wonder," said Father, "where Callum and the German are now? Gone abroad perhaps. Imagine having such power and using it for revenge against Sandy's mother. Just because she had a girl instead of a boy."

Father's face turned towards Marion, but his eyes stayed shut. "D'you think he knew George was Sandy's father? I expect he wouldn't have cared much. More obsessed with having a son for his experiments. Might be worth investigating that. Though I don't see why a girl shouldn't develop telekinesis. . ."

Marion allowed herself a smile.

Father stretched his face to the sun.

"I suppose," murmured Father, "this was a good out of the way place. With the privacy of a castle that no one visited. And very convenient that Lady Ferguson was Callum's grandmother. Probably thought she would never give them away. Ha! D'you remember Derek in a fury because Callum's party was cancelled!"

Father sighed. He murmured, "And that circle. Its energy vibrating at psychic levels, frightening the wild life. Destroying some of it.

I wonder if the German actually could have extended his own lifespan. It certainly gave him and Callum the power to move the gargoyle. How many people would they have scared to death...? Oh, well." Father breathed slowly. "It would've been no use telling the police. We couldn't have proved anything. And I still think —"

"Oh, go away!" smiled Marion. She didn't want to hear again, about Father's missed opportunity to study advanced telekinesis.

She was glad the German had lost his power. George certainly had whacked him with the clothes pole.

And she was glad Callum had lost *his* power. He was ugly-minded and would have been dangerous.

Poor Father had puzzled over why Callum's ability had gone.

Perhaps, one day soon, she would tell him.

She glanced towards the house.

Sandy, her hair bouncing with curls, was gloating over a tray of cakes with Mother and Derek.

Marion looked at Father.

His eyes were shut.

She stared at plums bunched above her on a branch.

She closed her mind around one plum, and tugged.

It fell into her lap.

WHY WEEPS THE BROGAN?
Hugh Scott

WED. 4 YEARS 81 DAYS FROM HOSTILITIES ... so reads the date on the clock in central hall.

For Saxon and Gilbert, though, it's just another day in their ritualized indoor existence. Saxon bakes, Gilbert brushes, together they visit the Irradiated Food Store, guarding against spiders. Among the dusty display cases, however, a far more disturbing creature moves...

But what *is* the Brogan? And why does it weep?

"Deftly evoked, the narrative is cleverly constructed, and there is no denying the nightmarish power of the story. There is a true shock ending." *The Listener*

"A very compelling and very interesting book."
Jill Paton Walsh
The Times Educational Supplement

A Whitbread Novel Award-winner
Shortlisted for the McVitie's Prize

THE PLACE BETWEEN
Hugh Scott

"Don't you know The Place Between? That's what I call it... In the darkness, there is somewhere else that comes between me and this world."

Waking late at night, Stella discovers her friend Daniel at her door, terrified, pleading to be let in. The fearful scratching sounds that follow give credence to his tale of haunted woods and creepy scrabbling twigs. Events quickly become even more sinister and dramatic, until there seems to be only one conclusion: some weird supernatural power is at work. A power that threatens to consume anyone in its path...

"Hugh Scott is a master of the genre."
The Sunday Telegraph

SOMETHING WATCHING
Hugh Scott

Beyond the table, something reared. Two tiny dots of light stared at Alice. The thing had grown. In its blackness she saw faint patterns of paw prints on sand...

Alice first sees the leopard-skin coat when her mother is clearing out the loft, ready for the family's move to an old castle – and it makes her shudder. Attached to the coat is a label insisting that it be burned, but without explanation. It soon becomes obvious, though, that something evil has been unleashed. Something monstrous. Something that means the family harm.

"A chilling tale in true gothic style, building to a spine-chilling climax." *The Times*